BOOK TWO – THE TATTOOED GIRL SERIES

# JANE of FIRE

## JESSICA PENOT

www.jessicapenot.com

Published Internationally by Jessica Penot
www.jessicapenot.com

Copyright © 2018 Jessica Penot

Exclusive cover © 2018 Fiona Jayde Media Designs
Interior design by Tamara Cribley www.deliberatepage.com

PRINT ISBN
978-1-7326928-3-1
EBOOK ISBN
978-1-7326928-2-4

Editor - Joanna D'Angelo
Copy Editor - Brenda Heald

*This book is dedicated to everyone who thinks they don't have enough strength inside themselves.*
*You do.*

# THANK YOU

Thank you to my talented publishing team - including Joanna D'Angelo, my editor and publishing coach; Tamara Cribley for her magical interior book design; and Fiona Jayde for her gorgeous cover. Thank you for helping me bring this book to fruition.

And to my readers, thank you for having faith in me. Every time you read one of my books, you tell me how much my stories mean to you.

**Let's keep in touch**
Sign up for my newsletter: Scary Girl News, and follow me on BookBub and Amazon for updates on my new releases and recommendations of books that I love. You can also find out more about me and my books and my spooky blog about real-life hauntings on my website: jessicapenot.com.

# MY BOOKS

**The Tattooed Girl Series:**
*Book 1 Jane of Air*
*Book 2 Jane of Fire*

Coming Soon:
*Book 3 Jane of Water*
*Book 4 Jane of Earth*
*Book 5 Jane of Darkness*
*Book 6 Jane of Light*

**The Accidental Witch Series:**
*Book 1 The Accidental Witch*
*Book 2 The Darkest Art*

**Single Titles:**
*Circe*
*Death's Dream Kingdom*
*The Monster Hunter's Manual*

**Twilight Saint Series:**
*The Twilight Saint*

**Haunting Series:**
*Haunted Chattanooga*
*Haunted North Alabama*

# CHAPTER 1

*There are black zones of shadow close to
our daily paths, and now and then some evil
soul breaks a passage through.*

~ H.P. Lovecraft

HOPE IS A STRANGE FEELING. It can make you
believe that the most wonderful thing you want in the world
might actually be possible. But it can leave you vulnerable
to that very desire you so desperately cling to.

I held onto my hope for a couple of weeks. I didn't dare
ask Mrs. Fairfax when Edward was coming, but I watched
for him on the horizon.

Edward Rochester, Miss Adele's grandson, and heir
to Thornfield Hall.

I waited for him. I found myself spending more time
at Thornfield Hall, hoping he would walk in on me. I
sat in the library at Thornfield and studied for my finals
when I normally would have gone to the university library.
I spent every minute I could at Thornfield, but Edward
didn't come. I returned to my usual routine. I turned in

my term papers and completed my finals and Christmas Break came.

All the other students returned home. They went back to their loving families. The campus became a ghost town. I called Helen and went to her apartment, again, but no one answered the buzzer. I didn't bother calling Mrs. Blankenship. I'd called her just before Thanksgiving and she'd said very little on the phone. She just wished me well and told me not to come back for Christmas.

"There's nothing left here for you," she said in a faint, raspy voice. "You're better off staying where you are. Just get on with your life and leave me in peace."

I bit my lip. Mrs. Blankenship never wanted to see me again. We had never been close, but she was the closest thing to family I had. It was like a knife in my heart. I was used to the knife and I thought that the most tragic thing about being an orphan was that eventually, I would stop feeling anything at all. There is only so much hurt and loneliness one person can take.

"Please understand," she'd said. "I do care about you, Jane. I think you are a such a smart young woman and every day I'm amazed at what you've accomplished, but every time I see you I remember him and I remember our dream to have a baby together. I remember how that dream died and then how he died. I can't bear it anymore. I have to let you go."

I'd wiped the tears from my eyes. I understood. I wanted Mrs. Blankenship to be happy. She'd been a shadow of a person for many years.

I tried Helen again, but there was no answer. I took a deep breath. I had spent many lonely Christmases growing up. Nothing had changed that much. It was late at night and the wind howled. The howling echoed throughout Thornfield's empty halls. The staff had put up a large Christmas tree in the foyer and a small one in the sitting room by Miss Adele's room. I sat in that sitting room in the glow of the little tree. I hadn't had a Christmas tree in years, not since Mr. Blankenship died. The twinkling lights lifted my spirits. It was cold outside and the night was dark. The moon was hidden by clouds, but I went to bed singing Christmas carols in my head.

I woke up early and ate breakfast with the staff. Mrs. Fairfax, Jenna, James, and the eternally expanding nursing staff that had stayed on through the holidays. There were four nurses who took turns taking care of Miss Adele during the day, by that point. Mrs. Fairfax played Christmas carols over breakfast and Miss Adele hummed along with them as she ate her oatmeal. Her hands shook as she tried to get the spoon to her mouth and the nurse had to help her eat. Miss Adele smiled at me.

"Edward will be here today," Mrs. Fairfax said to Miss Adele. "That's good news, isn't it?"

Miss Adele smiled broadly. "I knew he would come. I knew he would come."

"We'll be working hard today to get things ready for him," she said. "He'll be bringing his friend, Blanche, with him."

My heart sank a little to hear the beautiful blonde would be with him.

Jenna got up and dusted the crumbs off her pants. "Well, we better get to it then. The sooner we start the sooner we'll be done. That boy eats more than a herd of buffalo." Jenna headed over to the kitchen. I never did ask Jenna what she'd meant that night when she warned me to be careful with Edward. But after meeting Blanche, I'd pretty much figured it out. Edward was rich and gorgeous, and girls were drawn to him like bees to honey. He could never be with someone like me and I was foolish for letting myself even think it.

Mrs. Fairfax got up as the doorbell rang. I had to assume it was the cleaning crew to prepare the house. I helped the nurse with Miss Adele, who was still humming even after the music was turned off. I gave the nurse a little break and took Miss Adele down to the library. She picked a book off the shelf and sat with it in her lap, but she wasn't really reading. She was staring out the window.

"Are you okay?" I asked her.

"My Edward will love me, now," she said. "He'll love me, now, because I'm going to fix it."

I put my hand on Miss Adele's. "He's always loved you. He's coming home for Christmas, isn't he?"

"No, no," Miss Adele muttered softly. "No, no. Not my grandson. Not him. He has always loved me. No, my Edward will forgive me. My husband. Edward Rochester, X."

"I thought he'd passed away," I asked.

"People never really die here," she said. "They just wait. They wait here forever."

"No," I said. "They've gone to Heaven. Your Edward is waiting for you in Heaven."

Miss Adele shook her head. "There is no Heaven for us. We are hollow inside. There is no place for us in Heaven. We will stay on here until there is nothing left and, after that, who knows?" She began to hum and rub her hands together. "But it doesn't matter anymore, does it, Jane? I see what you are. This will all end soon."

"What am I?" I asked. I felt strangely shaken. People always asked me what I was. No one had ever told me what I was. The reversal in the phrase was disturbing. I knew she was just babbling nonsense, but her words resonated with me. "What do you think I am?"

"You are one of them. You are one of the others. You are Jane Air. You will fill us up and we won't be hollow anymore. You will set us all free. All the doors will open and the spirits will join us, here, and there will be bright days and fairy kings and queens will dance into the night with the goblin princes. All the world will turn to magic and ghosts will become flesh. There is a door on your back and when it opens, we will all be whole. You will see."

She smiled like she was talking about some wonderful recipe she had found for a casserole. She had completely lost her mind. How in the world did she know about my tattoo? Had she seen it one night when I was tending her in her room? No matter. I would have to talk to Edward about putting her in a nursing home since Mrs. Fairfax wouldn't hear of it.

I turned away from Miss Adele and looked out the window. A fog had settled over the gardens of Thornfield and it had begun to sleet. It was dark and I could barely see the car come down the driveway. It took its time creeping down to the house. It parked in front of the house and Edward stepped out, the fog wrapping around him like it longed for his touch. The wind blew his short, black hair. He was wearing a suit, as always. His blue-green eyes looked up at Thornfield like the house was his enemy. He stood there for a while, studying Thornfield, with his hands in his pockets. Finally, Blanche emerged from the car and scampered into the house, leaving Edward alone. It took him quite a while to walk into the house. A man I didn't know followed behind him with the luggage.

Miss Adele stopped humming and her eyes grew moist with tears. Her book fell from her hands. She was facing away from the window, but it was as if she could see everything I was seeing. She suddenly seemed very aware and very awake. She stood up and smoothed her pants out with her hands and straightened her hair.

Edward walked in with Blanche on his arm. He looked just as I had remembered him. I wanted to stare at him. I wanted to lose myself in him, but I looked down at my feet instead.

Edward didn't look at me. He just stared at his grandmother. "I'm here," he said.

"I need to speak with you, alone," Miss Adele said clearly.

"Wait here," Edward said to Blanche.

Blanche sat down and glared at me. She didn't say anything. It was clear she thought I wasn't worth her time. She just sighed and threw her leg over the arm of the chair. "What a bore," she muttered to herself. She took her cell phone out of her purse and began texting or playing a game or doing whatever it was people did with smartphones. I didn't really know since my phone was a prepaid phone from the grocery store that had cost me about thirty dollars. It didn't even take pictures. I returned to my book, but I was having great difficulty focusing.

Edward and Miss Adele were gone for what seemed like an eternity. Blanche sighed and played games and paced while she waited. Occasionally she would mutter something like, "Could this place be any more boring?" Mostly she just sighed and looked beautiful and bored.

The nurse came in and sat with me and waited for Edward. The three of us, together, were perhaps the most uncomfortable trio in existence. The nurse occasionally attempted small talk, but Blanche just shriveled her nose in disgust and I didn't know what to say to the nurse, so uncomfortable silence reigned.

When Edward and Miss Adele finally did return, he deposited his grandmother in the library like a prison guard returning a prisoner to their cell and grabbed Blanche and left. I took a deep breath. He hadn't even noticed me. The withering gaze that had once terrified and thrilled me was gone. He didn't even know I existed. The nurse was with Miss Adele, so I wandered away. I put on my coat and walked through the cold fog. I let the freezing rain sting my cheeks. The wind cut through my cheap raincoat and I was soaked to the bone, but I kept walking. I let the cold seep in and cut through me. I wanted to feel anything but the relentless pressure that was compressing my heart like a vice. I wanted to cut my heart out and leave it in the cold so I could never feel again. What use was feeling? These many weeks that Edward had been away, I had cobbled a happy enough existence with my life. I was busy at school and with my weekly Haiti group meetings. I was even starting to accept that Helen had left and wasn't coming back. Maybe she and Jake had eloped somewhere and she'd quit school. But now, after seeing Edward again, and being so completely ignored by him, I just felt broken. I longed for the cold to wash through me and freeze every part of me that had ever felt anything. I imagined that I was feeling what Liliana must have felt when she climbed her way up to Witching Hill to find her dark lord.

# CHAPTER 2

*There be those who say that things and places have souls and there be those who say they have not; I dare not say, myself.*

~ H.P. Lovecraft

BY THE TIME I GOT back, it was well past dark. The days had grown short and dinner was done. I was shaking. I couldn't feel my nose. My teeth chattered and I stumbled upstairs with the singular goal of getting out of my wet clothes, but I never made it to my room.

Edward was sitting in Miss Adele's sitting room waiting for me. He jumped up when he saw me and met me in the hall.

"Strange weather for a walk," he commented.

Despite the cold and the fact that I was dripping onto the hardwood floor, I managed a smile. He hadn't forgotten about me. He went and got me a blanket and put it over my shoulders. It didn't help much. I was still freezing, but I leaned into him as he drew the blanket around me. He was warm and his arms were strong. I stopped shaking and he let me go. I returned to my shaking.

"Come sit by the fire with me," he said, and I followed him into the sitting room. He put a chair by the fire for me and I put my hands near the warmth of the flames. I felt the sensation return to my fingers as warmth spread through them. My shaking began to slow.

"You must be very committed to exercise," he said. He was staring at me again. I had missed that. I missed the way he looked at me. It terrified me, but I loved it.

"I just needed some fresh air."

He smiled. His smile was so rare. He let go of his scowl and his face lit up. "Fresh air?"

I shrugged.

He got up and brought me another blanket. He kneeled in front of me and put the blanket on my lap. His hands lingered on me as he laid the blanket over me. "You'll catch your death out there," he said softly. He was still in front of me. I met his eyes. His blue eyes laced with green. They were dark around the edges and light in the middle, with flecks of green. They were beautiful. He pushed a lock of wet hair out of my face.

He got up and moved back to his chair. His shirt was wet. I was so wet that I had dripped on him. He didn't seem to care. The firelight cast strange shadows on his face. I was happy just to sit and look at him.

"How's school?" he asked.

"Wonderful," I said. "I got all As and I joined a pre-med mission club. We're going to Haiti, in the summer, to take care of the poor."

"I would expect nothing less than all As from you and the mission work sounds about right, too. How's college life. Going to lots of parties?"

I laughed. "Remember? Parties aren't my thing."

He smiled again. His entire face lit up. "I know. I was just kidding. I can't imagine you wasting your time with that crap."

"I don't think it's crap. I know a lot of very smart people who go to keggers and frat parties on the weekends. I just don't enjoy them. I wish I did. It would be nice to be like everyone else."

"Why would you like to be like everyone else? Why do you keep saying that?"

"I don't know. It would be nice to be like your Blanche. She seems so happy. She's just happy, dancing and talking about nonsense with everyone around her. It would be simpler being like everyone else, wouldn't it?"

"It would be simpler, but I don't think it would be better. You should stay the way you are. Blanche will never go to missions in Haiti or save another human life. She'll never make the world a better place. You'll do all those things."

I blushed. "You give me far more credit than I deserve. I haven't done anything, yet, and you never know what the future holds. Blanche may accomplish far more than me in the end. She is young. People grow and change."

Edward laughed. "It is good to see you, Jane."

My blush deepened.

"You are shivering. I suck. I stopped you from getting into dry clothes. Go, change. Dry off. I've saved you some dinner. Maybe we can talk more while you eat. I would love to see if I can beat you at chess."

"I would like that very much."

I went to my room and took off my clothes and dried off. I put on some jeans and an old sweater. I wished I had something pretty to wear. I wished I could find some way to make myself into one of the girls that men noticed, but my wardrobe was as lacking as my beauty. I walked back to the sitting room. Edward was still there. He'd laid the dinner out on the coffee table. It looked delicious. Jenna was an artist. Usually, Jenna cooked simple things for Adele and the staff, but when Edward came back her true gift was revealed. The flaky bacon and mushroom tart in front of me was a work of art.

"How was Yale?" I asked.

"Crowded," he answered.

"I thought all your friends were there. Do you wish you were there?"

"Not at all. I am sick of my friends. I really wish I was at my townhouse in New York. It is beautiful this time of year. Although, I think here might be better, now."

"You don't want to be in New York?"

"Sometimes. It definitely has its moments. I love going to concerts and I love the museums. The architecture is brilliant. Just walking through some neighborhoods is like exploring an art museum. I love the city at night when the lights come on and everything is buzzing. Anything seems possible then."

"So, you do love it?"

"I do."

"Is that why you avoid being here?"

Edward pointed to my plate. "Your food is getting cold."

I took a butter roll, broke it into pieces, and ate it. Edward watched me eat. "My grandmother loves you."

"That is very sweet," I said. "I wish I could do more for her. I need to talk to you about her. I'm getting worried that she's getting much worse."

"You're taking good care of her and we can talk about my grandmother in the morning," he said as he poured me a glass of wine. I had never had wine before. I didn't like to have my senses addled and I was far too young to drink, but I couldn't see the harm in a few sips. I took a sip and then another and before I knew it I had finished the glass. The wine warmed me and loosened my tongue.

"Can I ask you a strange question?" I asked, as he poured me another glass.

"I love strange questions."

"Do you ever hear laughing late at night?"

Edward frowned. "That's nothing. There's an old groundskeeper who spends the night here sometimes. Her name is Mrs. Pool. Sometimes she drinks too much and takes to laughing."

"Really? Why haven't I ever seen her?"

"She's a recluse."

I finished my food and looked up at him. He seemed happy in the warmth of the fire. I had never seen him really happy before. He looked younger when he was happy. He looked his age. I leaned back in my chair and basked in the heat. I stretched out my legs and smiled. The warmth of the fire filled me up so that I felt like a cup brimming with contentment. I poured myself another glass of wine.

"Where's your Blanche? Won't she miss you?" I asked.

"She left. She can't stand small towns. She says they're boring."

"She just abandoned you? At Christmas? She didn't stay long. Won't you miss her?"

Edward's smile melted and his typical scowl returned. "I think I can manage without her."

I thought, maybe, he was being sarcastic, but I wasn't sure. The wine had gone to my head and I felt a little out of it. The room was spinning and it seemed like Edward was the center of the vortex.

"She's so gorgeous," I said.

"There's more to beauty than a perfect body and a pretty face."

I laughed so hard I spilled some of my wine. "Really?! Not according to every fashion magazine and movie in existence."

Edward stood up and moved closer to me. "I shouldn't have given you wine. I'm sorry about that. You look like you weigh less than a blade of grass. The wine must have gone right to your head. Your cheeks are red. Are you okay?"

I grinned at him like a fool. "I'm fabulous. I'm wonderful. I haven't had a Christmas tree since I was little. I'm in a beautiful house, a mansion, with a beautiful tree, sure maybe the house is haunted as hell, and I kind of think the devil may be hanging out in the attic, and maybe the house was cursed by a beautiful witch who I really like even though she ate someone's eyes, but it is still wonderful here and I am even spending the night with the most beautiful guy I have ever seen. I would never have thought that was even possible..." I giggled like a silly girl.

Edward cupped my face with his hand and I melted into his arms. "You are beautiful too, Jane. You know that, don't you? You are so much more beautiful than Blanche because you are beautiful inside and out."

I giggled, again, and punched him in the shoulder. "I really like you. We should make-out. I have never made out."

Edward released me and walked across the room. I collapsed and lay on the sofa. The entire room was spinning around me in a maddening spiral.

Edward came back and handed me a glass of water and an Advil. I took it and looked up into his eyes. He could have done anything he wanted to me, at that moment. All my walls had vanished with the wine.

"I'm going to help you to bed," Edward said.

"Thank you," I whispered.

"I'm sorry. I didn't know you weren't used to drinking."

"*Yoooo don' know that.*" My speech was ridiculous and slurred. "*I could huuve had lozzzzz to drink before. I could be a-a- l-lushshsh for all yooo know.*"

"You're definitely not a lush. It probably doesn't help that you weigh about as much as a wet rat."

"*Are yooo s-saying I'm t-too skinny?*" I asked as he pulled me to my feet. "*I've always been t-too skinny. My f-foster mom used t' say I looked like a pole with hair. People always s-say*

15

*yoooo can never be toooo rich or toooo thin, but I've proven them wrong...WRONG! Well on the thin thing at least...I wish I had boobs. Men like boobs."*

"Wow. You are really drunk. You are fine. You look perfect."

I put my arm around Edward's waist and he walked me to my room. I loved feeling him near me. I looked at his neck. It is strange, the things you notice when you really study someone. He had a beautiful neck. I even loved the shape of his Adam's apple. He helped me to my bed and I collapsed.

"Did you know that your family was cursed?" I asked as I looked up at him.

"What?" he asked.

"I found these letters. They were tattered and torn and worn down with time, but they were lovely. I mounted them on special paper so time couldn't damage them anymore, and then I read them. A woman named Liliana loved one of your ancestors, but fate kept them apart, so she cursed your family forever. Did you know that? She sold her soul to the devil and she thought that she made your ancestor out of her own blood. You don't even have a soul. That is what the letters say."

Edward was silent. He reached down and touched my cheek. I grabbed his hand and held it for a minute. "Do you believe your family is cursed? Is that why all the girls you date die? Do you think the curse kills any girl you love?"

Edward pulled the covers over me. "My parents believed it. That was all that mattered. My grandmother still believes it."

16

"But you don't believe it?"

"It doesn't matter anymore."

"How can it not matter?"

"Because my grandmother says that the curse has ended and that I am free of it."

I let go of his hand and fell asleep almost immediately.

# CHAPTER 3

*Whatever our souls are made of, his and mine are the same.*

~ Emily Bronte

I STAYED IN MY ROOM for a long time the next morning. I remembered just enough of the previous night to be too embarrassed to want to see Edward again. I had to decide how to interact with Edward. I knew my feelings for him and the wine had made me say and do things I would never have done in any other circumstances. I wished I could take back the night before, but it was too late for that. I decided to apologize for my behavior to Edward, if I saw him, and give him the letters. I didn't assume I would see him. He had already spoken with his grandmother and Blanche was gone, so there was no reason for him to stay.

Mrs. Fairfax was in the front parlor decorating another Christmas tree and singing carols very loudly. She was covering the tree in small glass balls. The tree was already lit up and strands of popcorn hung from the branches. She sang *Silent Night*.

"Another tree?" I asked.

"Oh yes," she answered. "Edward is staying through the New Year. He wants to celebrate the holidays here."

I put my hand over my mouth to cover the smile that I couldn't suppress. "Will his friends be here with him?"

"No," Mrs. Fairfax answered. "It's a bit odd, he's never stayed here for so long before, but I'm not one to look a gift horse in the mouth. It will be wonderful for Miss Adele to be with family during the holidays. She hasn't really been with family since her son died."

"When did he die?" I asked.

"He died a few years ago. He killed himself after his wife died. He couldn't handle her death. Funny thing. For years the two couldn't stand each other. They fought like cats and dogs and he cheated. Finally, they began to get along and she died. He killed himself two months later. It is a sad story. I think that is why Edward can be so mean sometimes."

"How did Edward's mother die?"

"We don't like to talk about that," Mrs. Fairfax said curtly. I wanted to comment that it was odd that open discussion of a suicide and cheating was absolutely fine, but whatever killed Edward's mother was off limits. I bit my tongue. I had stepped over enough lines in the last twenty-four hours.

Mrs. Fairfax returned to her singing and I wandered off. My faith in facts above superstition was beginning to dwindle. I tried to tell myself that ghosts and superstition were nonsense. There was no curse. All the death that surrounded

20

the Rochester family was pure coincidence, but the evidence was piling up. I scratched my arm. My tattoo was beginning to spread, again, and it was beginning to itch. The strangest creatures crept down my arm. Strange monsters with tentacles and horns danced together. The monsters weren't all ugly. Some were beautiful, but I didn't want them on me and their cold yellow eyes were beginning to give me nightmares. It was becoming harder to hide my tattoos and harder to convince myself that Helen was wrong. Every woman that came near a Rochester died. I could be next if I kept allowing myself to get closer to Edward. I should go. I should find a doctor and have him look at my back. But I wouldn't do any of those things. Even knowing that Edward was hollow and deadly, I was like a moth drawn to his flame. I couldn't stop myself.

I ran upstairs and tied my hair back, leaving a few curls to dangle in front of my face. I put on my nicest sweater, although it wasn't as nice as I would have liked, and I even put on a little lipstick. I smiled at myself in the mirror, but my smile quickly melted into a frown. Who was I kidding? The face that stared back at me was utterly ordinary. Even with the lipstick, I was drab. I was like a big brown shoe. I looked like a scrawny child playing dress up. I shook my head and reminded myself that Edward was dating Blanche. I reminded myself that I was plain and that men like Edward never noticed girls like me. I had no shape to my figure. I was slim and flat chested. To make things worse, I was utterly boring. I had never been anywhere or seen anything. All I knew of life I had learned from books. Not to mention the fact that I had gotten so drunk I had asked to make out with him the night before and his response had been to toss me in my bed and tell me to sober up. I wanted to punch myself.

Edward, on the other hand, was three years my senior. He had traveled and seen the world. He'd been with Blanche, who was gorgeous with a perfect body. He was rich and intelligent and completely beautiful. Guys like that didn't fall in love with girls like me. I knew that. I told myself that, even if Edward was cursed, I was safe. He would never love me, so I had nothing to fear.

I decided to take a walk to clear my head. The fresh air always did me good. I pulled on my big brown jacket and went out into the winter air. It was so cold, a light frost covered everything. The cold didn't faze me. I had my big boots on and my coat was more than warm enough. I trudged down the main driveway through the campus and into town. It was eerily quiet. Christmas lights and garlands decorated the quaint little main street, but the people were conspicuously absent. The little town almost ceased to function when the students were gone. I walked into a little coffee shop where I used to meet Sinjun, Sara, and Mary. I sat for a while drinking my coffee and trying to convince myself that I had to let go of my unrealistic dreams. I had to focus on what was real. I had to focus on school and put dreams of romance from my mind.

I walked back out into the cold, convinced I had succeeded in setting my mind straight. I thought about the classes I would take in the spring and the things I would do with the pre-med club. I was so lost in thought, I didn't even notice where I was walking. I just walked. I walked until I realized I was back at the stables. James was there, feeding the horses and talking to them. He had one horse saddled. James noticed me come in and smiled his creepy smile at me. I preferred the ghosts to his creepy smile.

James stopped feeding the horse and walked toward me. "You look nice," he said. He got so close I could feel his breath on my cheek. I tried to back away, but I had somehow backed myself into a corner.

"I don't look nice," I argued. "I look like a wet rat in a big coat."

James unzipped my jacket and moved in even closer if that was possible. His chest pressed against my breasts, and I was suddenly paralyzed. I couldn't move or breathe.

"Why haven't we hooked up?" he whispered into my ear.

"Y-you're making me uncomfortable. Please, let me go."

He laughed and squeezed my breast.

"What the hell are you doing, James?" Rage filled Edward's voice. I had never been so grateful to hear someone angry before in my life.

"Just making plans for later," James was still staring at me.

Edward grabbed James by the arm and threw him across the stables. I zipped my coat back up. I felt like one of those stupid, helpless girls from all the movies I hated. Why hadn't I punched James? Why had I needed Edward to save me? Tears burned in my eyes. James was on the ground and Edward hit him, hard.

James laughed at Edward. "Sorry. I didn't realize you were hitting that." I blushed when I realized that I was 'that.'

Edward hit him again. "You are fired. Get the hell out, before I kill you."

James stood up and wiped the blood from his nose. "Your loss, little Jane. You don't know what you're missing." James made an obscene gesture in my direction and then turned to Edward. "Good luck finding anyone who's willing to work in this horror show on short notice. Don't blame me if your damn horses starve." James stormed away.

I covered my face in shame. I had completely frozen like a coward. I hadn't done anything. I was still crying. I felt stupid and weak. I felt Edward's arms around me.

"Are you okay?" he asked. "I'm sorry. I had no idea he was such an asshole."

I squirmed out of Edward's arms. "I'm fine!" I yelled in a sudden fit of rage. "I have never felt so stupid in my life."

"Why?" Edward asked.

"I should have fought back." I wept.

"You were shocked. He weighs sixty pounds more than you. What could have you done?"

I shook my head. "I don't know. Anything. You must think I am a complete idiot. I got drunk and humiliated myself in front of you last night and now you find me letting some jerk fondle me in a stable."

"I don't think you're an idiot! I think you're wonderful!" Edward seemed surprised for once. He looked like he didn't know what to do. I had never seen him like this.

"Seriously?" I asked. "You think I'm wonderful?"

"Would you like to go for a ride?"

I nodded. "I would love to."

Edward saddled the horses for us and I pulled myself together while I watched him work. He helped me into the saddle, again. I felt more at ease this time. I knew the horse, Bella, from my first time out with Edward, and I knew she wouldn't hurt me. The ride was pleasant. The horse's feet crunched over dead leaves and frost as we walked. The sun warmed our backs and the world around us. We didn't talk about anything important. We talked about books and art and movies. He told me about London and his tour of the haunted London Tower. He also told me about Paris and Rome, and it was like I was going there myself. He spoke with such clarity that I could see the places in my mind's eye and imagined myself standing with him at the top of Notre Dame or on the road to Pere Lachaise.

We went to the same place we had gone to before. We went to the fire tower. I didn't hesitate to take his hand as he helped me up the rusty structure to the top. Together, we looked out on the world.

"This is the only place I have ever known peace," he said as he looked out.

"But you've been everywhere! You've seen such beauty. How can you not have known peace?" I asked.

"The past is a ghost I carry with me. There are very few places I can let my ghosts go and just be."

I nodded. "I know that feeling."

He touched my cheek. There was a tear on it. I hadn't even noticed it myself.

"You have as many ghosts as I do, don't you?"

"There are so many people in this life who have hurt far worse than me. I try not to focus on the dark parts of my life. I try to stay focused on the light ahead of me. I've been lucky in so many regards. If I focus on the past, I will be pulled down and it will drown me."

Edward's laughter was as bitter as the winter wind. "I wish I had your wisdom. Some days I think the past will drown me. Other days, I think it already has."

I put my hand on his shoulder and looked up at him. "Don't say that. You have so much to live for. I know your life has been hard. Death has surrounded you and taken many people you love, but you are still here and the sun is shining on you. You are rich and young and handsome. Life has given you so much others can only dream of. You have to remember that."

He placed his hand on mine and held it. I gazed into his blue eyes with flecks of green and couldn't breathe, they were so beautiful.

"And you have your Blanche, now," I added. "You aren't alone." Why did I say that? Why was I such a consistent, bumbling idiot? I blushed in anger. I was angry at myself.

He let go of my hand and turned away from me. "That's right. I have Blanche." His voice was hard and cold. "We should go now. It's getting late."

"Can I say something before we go?" I asked.

"Sure."

"I want to apologize for last night. I was too forward and I shouldn't have said anything I said. I can't believe I asked you to make out. I really am not like that. I was just drunk. I shouldn't have tortured you with questions about hearing laughter in the middle of the night and family curses. I would like to give you your family letters if you want them. I preserved them for you."

"It's okay," he said, turning back to me. "That damn curse has haunted me my entire life. It's good to talk about it. I'm sure most people would think my family was crazy, but the curse has always been very real to the Rochesters. Even if the curse was just a myth, it has still overshadowed all of our lives, for as long as I can remember. I would love to go through the letters with you."

"Are you sure you want to read the letters with me? They are…. Haunting. I almost believed in the curse after I was done with them. Maybe you have been through enough. Maybe you don't want me to read the letters with you."

"After my mother died," he said, "my father was so sure that he'd killed her. He said she turned to dust in his arms. He said that if he had just kept hating her she would have lived. He killed himself. He hung himself from the chandelier. What a cliché! I think my entire family is insane. My grandmother told me that it was my fault Bertha died. I had cared about her, so she died. I wasn't allowed to date, but I met Bertha at a coffee shop and I really liked her. She was a sweet girl. She was my first love. We made love in the stables on a warm, summer night. The next day things got weird. She started following me. She threatened to kill me. She talked about monsters and demons following us. Her parents took her for a psychiatric evaluation.

She killed herself. It was easy to believe my grandmother was right. It was my fault she died. There was another girl I liked. I didn't even like her that much, but she was hit by a car. My grandmother said that was my fault, too. She said I can only be with girls I hate. It is crazy. Living this way is a sign of mental illness, but I can't stop. I can't help thinking that the curse is real and that I am hollow, and if I let myself care about anyone, they will die. I am glad you found the letters. I am glad I can finally talk to someone about this. I have lived with this my entire life and I can never tell anyone. Do you have any idea how lonely that is?"

I had no idea what to say, so I took his hand in mine. He was shaking.

"I don't even remember my parents," I said. "I can't even remember my mother's name. I used to spend so much time conjuring up their images in my mind. I imagined they were rich and beautiful and perfect. I dreamed that I would end up like Oliver Twist and someday my long-lost relatives would find me and save me from my life, but they never came. I imagined so many stories about myself. I was a foundling like Heathcliff in *Wuthering Heights*. I just turned up on the floor in an Emergency Room. Someone had just thrown me down on the filthy floor and walked away. *Jane* was written on my head with a Sharpie. Even better than that, someone wrote some incredible bullshit on my chest: *Love is the gateway. Love is the key. Love is the door that will set all the old ones free.* That was on my chest! I was naked, so I am going to assume my family was completely insane, too..." I hadn't realized how much bitterness

28

had tainted my voice. I had told him almost everything, but I stopped just short of telling him about the tattoo. "I know what loneliness is."

"I am so sorry, Jane. I really am."

I shook my head. "I try not to think about it." I was trying not to cry. I was holding back my tears with everything I had in me.

Edward squeezed my hand and we stood together looking out on the beautiful world. We looked out over the rolling hills and the verdant forest. We looked out on the tiny town, nestled in the gentle slopes of the Appalachians. The sun went down in a swirling display of orange and purple, leaving only a sprinkling of stars behind it. Edward's hand was warm and strong in mine, and I wished the moment would never end.

# CHAPTER 4

*I will walk where my own nature
would be leading.*

~ Emily Bronte

ON THE RIDE HOME, I told Edward about the letters.
I told him about Liliana and her broken heart and about
her tragic end. He listened quietly. As we got off our horses,
he took my hand again.

"Maybe my family deserved the curse," he said. "Liliana
sounds terrifying. Maybe my ancestor should have just married her."

"You should read the letters, yourself. I'm filtering them
through my own bias. I don't want to say anything bad
about your family."

Edward laughed. "My feelings won't be hurt by your
calling my ancestors jerks. It was over 300 years ago."

I laughed, too. "I guess you're right. I hadn't thought
about it like that. I always thought big, rich families like
yours wanted to protect their family name going back to
the beginning of time."

"Maybe they used to. Maybe some people still think like that, but my family is so messed up, I can't even defend the actions of my own father. He hated my mother, you know. He was forced to marry her when he was very young. He could barely stand to look at her. Eventually, she grew to hate him, too. She lived on one side of Thornfield and he lived on the other side. It was the same with my grandparents. Grandma lived on your end of Thornfield and my grandfather lived on the end I'm in. They all hated each other and tortured each other in passive-aggressive ways. My father cheated. My mother drank. Then after they hated each other for so many years, they realized they loved each other and she ended up dying and then he killed himself. It's completely crazy. How could I possibly defend the honor of my family? The Rochester men have been sleeping with and marrying women they hate for generations. They do it on purpose. It is cruel."

I sat in the cold and watched Edward take the saddles off the horses and put them in the stables. It was too cold to leave them out. I sat by the heater in the barn and warmed my hands. Edward worked quickly and before I knew it we were walking again.

We walked back to Thornfield slowly. It was growing cold, again, and I shivered in my heavy coat. The wind blew and I felt like its icy breath would penetrate all the way down to my bones. By the time we made it back inside I was shivering. Edward walked me back to my room and I gave him the letters that I had mounted in the books.

"Thank you for this," he said as he held the books. "You have no idea how much this means to me."

"I'm glad I could help," I answered.

"Will I see you at dinner in an hour?"

"Definitely."

I cleaned up and changed my clothes. I put on more lipstick. I wanted to look my best for dinner. I helped the nurse walk Miss Adele to the dining room. Miss Adele was babbling and shaking. I couldn't really understand what she was talking about, but she kept saying burn under her breath. I tried to comfort her. I put my arm in hers for the walk down to the dining room. I told her Edward was staying for Christmas, but she seemed to only grow worse.

"Be careful," she said to me before we made it to the dining room. "Be careful, little bird. Don't get burnt. Don't get burnt, little bird. The fire is coming. It's coming. It will open. They are coming. The door will open. I can hear them. The old ones. I can feel them in my bones."

"It's okay," I said as I sat her down at the table. "There's no fire. There's only ice. Look," I said as I pointed to the window, "it's beginning to snow."

It snowed so rarely. We weren't far enough North to get heavy snow, so there was something magical in the white crystals that danced in the frigid air just outside the window. It was like something out of a fairy tale. I walked over to the window and watched the snow as it fell and cover the gardens in a pretty white blanket. It collected at the feet of old statues and trees and made mounds of white crystal where old leaves and weeds had once ruled. The Christmas lights shone out onto the snow, illuminating the white with shades of red and green. All was right with the world.

I sat next to Miss Adele during dinner and helped her eat. Her hands were shaking far too much for her even to attempt to feed herself. Edward and I had steak, but Miss Adele had soup. I carefully fed her each spoonful.

"I want my Edward," she said with soup dribbling down her chin. I wiped her mouth with the napkin. "Where is my grandson?" Adele pushed my hand away. "He said he'd come home."

"I'm here grandma," Edward said.

"No! No." Her hands began to shake and she picked up the bowl of soup and threw it across the room. "You aren't him. You are just trying to confuse me. Where is my Edward! He promised he'd come. I have to tell him something. I have to warn him."

Miss Adele hurled her salad plate against the wall and it shattered right next to the soup stain. The nurse took a syringe out of her fanny pack.

"Help me," the nurse ordered me. I helped hold Miss Adele while the nurse gave her an injection.

"Can't you smell the smoke!" Miss Adele began to yell. "Can't you smell it?" She grabbed my steak off my plate and threw it. "I want to go home! I want to go home! Why did I come here? Why did I come here? I want my mother! I don't want the old ones to come. I am afraid. I am afraid."

Edward got up and gathered his grandmother into his arms. He carried her like a baby, upstairs to her room. The nurse and I followed him. Miss Adele thrashed all the way and didn't calm down until Edward tucked her gently into her bed.

"It's all right now," Edward said to her. "I know now. Everything will change. The curse is over. Don't worry, Grandma. Don't worry. It's all over."

Slowly, Miss Adele calmed down and drifted off to sleep. The nurse sat on the bed beside Miss Adele and smoothed back her hair.

"She should be in a nursing home," the nurse said. "If you aren't willing to put her in a home, you should consider hospice. Home health can no longer provide her with the care she needs."

"Hospice?" Edward asked. "Isn't that for people who are dying?"

The nurse nodded and handed Edward a card.

"Think about it and we can discuss it more in the morning," the nurse said.

Edward and I left the nurse to her duties. We returned to our meals. Jenna and Mrs. Fairfax were frantically trying to clean the mess Miss Adele had left. I had a fresh steak on my plate. With Miss Adele gone, Edward seemed impossibly far away, so he picked up his plate and took the seat that had once been occupied by his grandmother. We sat next to each other. We were so close our arms brushed while we were eating. The room was lit by candlelight and the snow fell outside in huge fluffy flakes. Mrs. Fairfax and Jenna left and I was alone, with Edward, in the candlelight.

We ate silently. I knew that what the nurse had said was weighing on his mind. I agreed with the nurse. Miss Adele needed more care, but Edward had been gone so long he didn't know how bad his grandmother was getting. Dessert came and he and I ate French Silk pie together.

I followed him to Miss Adele's sitting room after dinner. He lit a fire and we sat together in silence for a while.

"Do you think she needs hospice?" he asked me.

"She needs more care than we can provide," I answered.

He nodded. "I wish there was a television with cable here. We've got to get cable or Wi-Fi or something."

"I like it better this way," I said. "Although, I would like to see a movie now and again."

"Would you like to go to a movie with me?" he asked.

"I would love that, but the nurse's shift is almost over and we can't leave your grandmother alone."

"A little money solves every problem. I'll just go bribe the nurse into staying later."

Edward vanished and when he returned he took me out in his Jaguar. I felt completely out of place in his fancy car. I felt like a scullery maid sitting in the king's carriage. I looked down at my hands. The nails were bitten down and scraggly. My boots were worn and scuffed and my jeans were faded. I felt like I was soiling the pristine leather of his beautiful car.

We went to see a comedy together. It was light and funny and full of jokes so inappropriate I couldn't help but laugh. He laughed, too, and for a minute we forgot about Miss Adele and everything sad that had shaped our lives. There was only laughter and jokes about farting.

# CHAPTER 5

*Every leaf speaks bliss to me
fluttering from the autumn tree.*

~ Emily Bronte

I THINK I WAS GLOWING the next morning. I was so happy, there were no words. I went downstairs early for breakfast and ate with the rest of the staff. I grinned stupidly as I ate my oatmeal and then helped the nurse feed Miss Adele. She never ate for the nurses.

After breakfast, I headed back up to Miss Adele's sitting room, hoping I might find Edward there waiting for me. Instead, I found Mrs. Fairfax. She was sitting in front of the fire, with knitting needles and yarn in her lap. She knit as she spoke.

"You don't have a mother, do you?" Mrs. Fairfax said as I walked into the room.

"No," I answered. "I'm an orphan."

"I have grown quite fond of you, Jane, and I'm going to give you the advice any loving mother would give her daughter in this circumstance."

"What's that?" I asked.

"Be careful. You are very young and you don't know much of the world or of men. I can see what's happening between you and Edward and I think you should guard your heart and your body. I would hate to see either ruined or broken."

"I appreciate the advice, but I'm no fool. There is nothing between Edward and me, and even if there were, I doubt he would do anything to ruin or break any part of me. He's a good guy. He would never hurt me."

"There is so much you don't know. You are just a girl. I have lived far longer than you and I am wiser than I look. I know men. Be careful."

"I'm always careful," I said.

"Stay away from Edward. He can hurt you in a way that can never be healed."

I shook my head. I couldn't imagine Edward hurting anyone or anything. I didn't care about curses. I turned and left Mrs. Fairfax to her knitting and bumped into Edward in the hall. He was dressed casually, again. I liked him in jeans.

"Would you like to go on an adventure?" he asked.

I nodded and he pulled me away from Thornfield Hall. He took me on a car ride, through the mountains into the woods. He took me far from home to a place where waterfalls danced over babbling brooks. We walked up into the mountains, past the frigid streams, and into a place where the trees were so thick you could get lost ten feet from your destination. Snow hung on the branches of the trees and covered the forest floor.

He pulled me upward as if we were climbing to reach the face of God. We were too out of breath to talk, but he was always in front of me, helping me and pulling me on. It was cold, and the higher we got the colder it became. At the top of the mountain, the snow on the ground was thick and icicles hung from every tree. They hung from the branches like tinsel clinging to Mrs. Fairfax's Christmas tree.

I stood on the top of the mountain and looked down on the world far below. I shivered as a cloud passed the sun and the wind pulled my hat from my head. My hair spilled out and became tangled in the wind.

Edward handed me his hat. "But you'll get cold," I said.

He pulled the hat over my head. "I like the cold."

The view from the mountain top was one of the most beautiful things I had ever seen. The world was covered in snow. It lay on top of the landscape turning the world white. Everything seemed so far away, so peaceful. It was sublime. The view was worth the climb. It was worth the breathless scramble upward.

"Do you spend a lot of time climbing?" I asked as I looked at Edward. He seemed so peaceful, so happy.

"No," he said. "I used to when I was a boy growing up here, but after my parents died, everything changed."

He turned to me. "How about you, Jane?" he asked. His eyes were staring into mine with that intense look that I loved. "Have you ever been on the top of a mountain?"

"No," I said. "I'm boring. This is the farthest I've ever been from home."

"You belong here; you know that? There is something about you that fits in with all of this natural beauty."

I moved away from him. I put my feet on the edge of a precipice that looked out over the valley. I leaned into the wind and let it tangle my hair and pull at my scarf. The air was fresh and clean and smelled of campfire and old leaves. The warm sun bathed my face in heat and the wind pushed the heat away and cooled me.

"We should go back," I said. I turned and started back down the mountain. He let me lead the way on the journey. He followed silently behind me.

We returned to Thornfield just before dark and were greeted by Mrs. Fairfax. She seemed worried. She told Edward that there was a gentleman waiting for him in the study. Edward and I made our way there. A fire danced in the stone fireplace and a thin, red-haired man sat in the large leather armchair by the fire. He looked like he was in his late twenties.

The smile vanished from Edward's face and the scowl, I had gotten to know so well in our first encounters, replaced it. Edward turned to me.

"Leave," he growled at me.

I looked at him for a minute. I was stunned. I hadn't expected his harshness. He had been so kind and I had begun to feel like we were good friends.

"Are you deaf!" he yelled at me. "I said you need to leave."

I turned and ran from the room. I fled upstairs to my bedroom and fell onto my bed. I buried my face in the pillow. I wondered if I'd ever know what to expect from Edward and his ever-changing moods. As soon as I thought I knew him, he changed.

I ate dinner with Miss Adele and Mrs. Fairfax. Edward didn't join us. The nurse took the evening off. It was getting harder and harder to find nurses that were willing to work with Miss Adele. As I tried to feed her that night, the soup dripped from her mouth onto her lap. She didn't even seem to understand how to chew or swallow her meal. She looked at me blankly. She didn't speak anymore and when she did she only talked about fire. *The fire is coming. Let it all burn. Let it all burn. Let it all burn.* She was like a metronome.

Mrs. Fairfax cleaned up after dinner and I took care of Miss Adele. I gave her a sponge bath and brushed her thinning hair. I cleaned her dentures and helped her into her pajamas. She didn't fight me. She was calm, but no one was home inside her head. She just stared into vacant space. I gave her the drug-laced tea and she was able to swallow most of it. I put her to bed and she just stared at the ceiling. She seemed catatonic. I didn't know much about medicine. I wasn't even a med student yet, but I knew her decline from semi-functional to completely catatonic was odd. I wondered why the nurses hadn't noticed.

I crawled into bed with my favorite Christmas book, *A Christmas Carol*. I drifted away into the novel. I was so lost in the story that I didn't hear the yelling, at first. It was the thump that roused me. I sat up. There was another thump and then a shout that sent shivers down my spine. I got out of bed and ran toward the yell. I stumbled through the halls and up into the red tower where I'd found Edward's girlfriend's journal. I burst into the room.

# CHAPTER 6

*Any relic of the dead is precious,*
*if they were valued living.*

~ Emily Bronte

THE MAN WHO HAD COME to see Edward was lying
on the bed. His shirt was torn and soaked in blood. Blood
covered him and the floor. Edward was holding a towel over
the man's abdomen. The man was yelling in unspeakable
pain. He was a mangled mess. I took a deep breath and ran
to Edward's side. I took the towel from him and put pressure on the wound. Edward looked panicked. He clearly
didn't know what to do. Calm spread over me.

"Elevate his legs," I said. "And call an ambulance
quickly."

I grabbed a couple of pillows and put them under the
man's legs and told Edward to call 9-1-1. I was left alone
with the blood-soaked man, putting as much pressure on
his wound as I could. The man yelled, again, and I grabbed
a pillow from the bed and switched from the towel to the
pillow. The towel was so saturated with blood it wouldn't

stop the blood flow anymore. The man grabbed my arm and looked at me with wild green eyes.

"It's all right," I promised him. "The ambulance will be here soon."

He slid his hand down my arm and put his hand in mine. He squeezed it as tightly as he could and I squeezed back. "Don't leave me alone," he said. "I don't want to die here. Stay with me."

"You aren't going to die," I said. "The wound hasn't hit any major organs. The abdomen is just profusely vascularized and has an extraordinary number of nerves in it. It is going to hurt like fire, but you won't die. The paramedics are on their way."

"Hold me," he yelled.

I pulled his head onto my lap and continued applying pressure to his wound. He squeezed my hand so tightly I thought I might lose blood flow in it. He started shaking and yelling again, and I did the only thing I could. I kept pressure on the wound and held his hand. I let him scream and carry on. "There is something here!" he wailed. "It isn't human. It isn't human. It has my sister. The monster has my sister. She is trapped. Help me!"

Edward came up the stairs with the paramedics. One of the paramedics pushed me out of the way and took over. He began working on the wound and a second paramedic started an IV. The man calmed down very quickly.

"What happened?" the second paramedic asked.

"He fell," Edward answered.

The paramedic looked incredulous. "This doesn't look like a fall. It looks like he was mauled by a tiger."

"It was a bad fall," Edward said.

"My sister!" the man cried out. "It has my sister! Please God! Please! It will kill us all."

"His sister is dead," Edward said. "He must be delirious."

"Bertha! Bertha!" he yelled.

One of the paramedics gave him a shot of something and he stopped thrashing and screaming. He fell asleep quickly and they carried him out on the stretcher. Edward and I followed behind the paramedics and helped them navigate the labyrinth that was Thornfield.

When the paramedics drove away, I became aware that I was standing in the foyer in nothing but a blood-soaked t-shirt. I felt cold and naked. I squirmed to make sure my shirt covered my tattoo. Edward must have seen me squirming because he quickly wrapped his jacket around my shoulders.

"What happened?" I asked into the cold

"He fell," Edward said.

"I can't believe that," I said.

"He fell down the stairs and gashed his side on a nail."

I turned to Edward. I was too tired to deal with mysteries and lies. "I think I'm going to bed."

He reached out and grabbed my hand. He had blood all over him and it was dripping from his shirt and pooling at my toes. I knew, in that moment, that he really wanted me. I saw the longing in his eyes and I drew back. I pulled away from him in fear. I didn't want to die. Superstition and fear drove me. In that moment, I was really afraid of the curse and I was afraid of myself.

"Stay with me," he said.

"I'm cold," I answered.

He let go of my hand and I walked back upstairs to my room. I showered and washed the blood from me and put on a flannel nightgown. I crawled into bed and grabbed the old journal I had found in the tower room. Bertha's journal. I closed my eyes and I could still hear that man screaming. I could hear him screaming her name, over and over again.

The Rochester curse had killed his sister.

# CHAPTER 7

*Life is a hideous thing, and from the background behind what we know of it pure daemoniacal hints of truth which make it sometimes a thousandfold more hideous.*

~ H. P. Lovecraft

THE NEXT MORNING, I WAITED for Edward in the sitting room. I wanted to talk to him about what had happened in the night. I needed him to make sense of it. I just couldn't believe the man's wound had come from falling down the stairs. I didn't wait long before Mrs. Fairfax emerged from the hallway.

"I knew you'd be here," she commented. "Edward wanted me to let you know that he had to go to the airport to get Blanche. Also, someone called looking for you. They said you weren't answering your cell phone. I took a message."

She handed me a plain white slip of paper. I took it and read the words carefully. Mrs. Blankenship was dying. She wanted to see me before she left this world. She had been trying to call me. I took my phone out of my pocket and looked at it. I wondered how long the battery had been dead and slipped the phone back in my pocket.

I thought of Helen as I packed my bag to go home. I remembered our journey to Thornfield together. I missed her so much it hurt. I didn't know what I had done to deserve her abandoning me, but it didn't even matter. She was gone and Edward was off picking his girlfriend up from the airport. I was alone. I had to remember that.

I waited for Edward to return and caught up with him when he was alone. Blanche was resting and I found Edward in the library looking through the journal of letters I had given him. He was studying the notes carefully. His eyes lingered on each page the way a lover might linger over a kiss. I hated to interrupt him, but time was of the essence.

"I'm sorry to bother you," I said as I approached him.

Edward looked up at me. His face was creased with worry. His mouth was twisted in anger and his eyes shone with some violent emotion I didn't understand. I stood back. His moods were like the winter weather and I wasn't sure I was strong enough to handle another of his storms.

"My foster mother has taken ill and I need to go home and visit her," I said.

He stood up and walked to me. It didn't matter that I had backed away, he put himself so close to me that we could have kissed. I met his gaze. I didn't want to back down from him anymore. I looked into his amazing blue-green eyes and held my ground.

"And what should I do while you're gone?" he asked.

"You could hire a temporary night companion for your grandmother or perhaps you could move down to her end of the hall to watch for her nightly wanderings. Maybe Blanche could help you."

"Don't you know there is no one else who could help me?"

"That's nonsense. Even Mrs. Fairfax could fill my position for a few nights while I go to stay with my foster mother."

"Go then," he said. He turned his back to me and went back to reading the letters.

"I haven't been paid this month," I said.

He took out his wallet and handed me a wad of cash. He grabbed my fingers and held them as the money passed into my hand. I pulled away from him. He was toying with me. How could he be so flirtatious with me when his girlfriend was napping upstairs? I flushed with anger and frustration. What was he doing? I looked at the stack of bills in my hand. They were all hundreds.

"This is far too much," I said.

He took the money back and handed me two 100-dollar bills.

"This isn't enough."

"You'll have to come back for the rest," he said.

I turned to leave, but he stopped me. He put his hand on my shoulder. I wanted to take his hand. I wanted to turn and throw myself into his arms, but I wouldn't be made into a fool. I wouldn't let him break my heart while his girlfriend was in the same house.

"Come back to me," he said as I walked away.

I had to jumpstart the Jeep. It had been so long since I had used it the battery had died. I had saved a significant amount of money by not driving. I threw my bag in the back of it and started my long journey home.

# CHAPTER 8

*The darkness always teemed with
unexplained sound - and yet he sometimes
shook with fear lest the noises he heard
subside and allow him to hear certain other
fainter noises which he suspected were
lurking behind them.*

~ H.P. Lovecraft

I DIDN'T GET TO SEE Mrs. Blankenship my first night
home. The hospice nurse, who was watching over her at
night, didn't want me to wake her. I settled myself into
my old bedroom. It wasn't as cold as it had been. Mrs.
Blankenship must have found some money. In fact, everything seemed better. Except for the stench of death in the
air, it could have been a happy home. There was food in
the cupboards and the fridge was full. All the lights were
on and the entire house was warm. It felt like the home I'd
wished for when I was living there.

I watched a couple of movies on cable before I went to
bed. I didn't realize how much I had missed real television

at Thornfield until I had it that night. I fell asleep with the
TV on in my room. It must have been well after 3 a.m.
when I woke up. The television was blaring. The screen was
filled with static. It was as if someone had suddenly turned
the volume up. I got out of bed and turned the television
off. It was freezing. I could see my breath in front of me.

I jumped back into bed and pulled the covers up to my
chin. I closed my eyes for a minute and then I felt someone's hand on mine. I opened my eyes and Helen was lying
next to me in the bed. She was curled up beside me under
the covers.

"Helen!" I cried out. I wrapped my arms around my
friend and hugged her tightly. "I'm so sorry! I'm so sorry. I'm
not sure what I did to drive you away, but I'll do whatever
I have to do to make things better between us."

Helen hugged me back. She squeezed me so tightly I
could barely breathe. "Forgive me," she said. "It wasn't you.
You're awesome. You know that. It was that place. I can't
see you anymore. Something isn't right."

I sat up and looked at Helen. "It scared you that much?"

Helen shrugged. "You know me. I'm not afraid of much,
but I can't go back there."

"I don't understand."

"Do you remember how we met?"

I tried to remember. It was strange. There was a blank
spot in my memory. I couldn't remember how I'd met
Helen. It was like she'd always been there. I didn't have
many memories without her. I knew that I hadn't met her
when I was at Mrs. Reed's house. Mrs. Reed had been my

second foster parent, just before Mrs. Blankenship and her husband. It was funny, but I couldn't remember my first foster home...I thought it was because I was so young...

Helen took my hand and held it warmly. I looked at her, into her beautiful blue eyes, and I started to remember...Those terrible memories I had made myself forget. I remembered things I loathed to think about. I saw my first foster father, Bob Ferguson. I saw his wicked sneer and greasy hair. He used to sit on the sofa with a beer balanced on his gut after dinner. He would look at me in a way that made me want to vanish. He would grin at me and tell me to sit on his lap. I never did, and he would get so mad. I remembered hiding in the closet when he got mad. He would lash out at everyone around him. I could hear my foster mother howling with rage as he hit her. She was no lamb and she'd hit back. I could hear things breaking. My foster mother was gone most of the time and when she wasn't there to abuse, Bob turned to us.

I'd always felt safe in that closet. I would hide behind a stack of old boxes. I knew no one would find me there, but I wasn't alone. I had never been alone in that closet. Helen was there. Helen and I sat in the back of the closet together. We'd hold hands. She'd had long hair then. It had been so pretty. I used to braid it for her. It was long and straight and silky and black. I could remember the day we cut it. She had come to me after school with tears in her eyes.

"Please help me," she'd said, weeping. "I don't want long hair anymore. You have to help me cut it. I have to cut it all off.

I never understood her then. Why would she want to cut her beautiful, long, black hair? I hadn't understood why anyone would want to be ugly when they were so beautiful, but I loved her. I loved her like a sister, so I helped her cut it. I took the scissors and cut it so short that she was almost bald. I cried and cried because it was so short, but she hugged me tight and told me it would be all right.

We tried to hide in the closet that night. She and I sat in the darkest part of our secret world, with our backs pressed up to the wood. We each held our stuffed animals in our arms. Helen told me we would always be together. Helen looked at me with such urgency. I could remember what she'd said: "Don't try to help me, Jane. No matter what happens, just cover your ears and don't try to help me. Stay in the closet. Stay hidden."

I opened my eyes and let the memories fade away. I didn't want to remember anymore. It hurt too much. "You were my foster sister," I whispered.

"I was," Helen said. Helen was crying. I could see tears flowing down her cheeks.

"Do you remember why they took you out of our house? Do you remember why you were moved?" Helen asked

I shook my head. "I don't want to remember anymore."

Helen ran her hand through my hair. "Jane, sweet Jane. You can't hide from the past forever. You have to remember now."

# CHAPTER 9

*Memories and possibilities are even
more hideous than realities.*

~ H.P. Lovecraft

THE MEMORIES WASHED OVER ME like a flood.
They came so quickly I thought I might drown in them.
They washed over me and pulled me back into that closet. I
was six years old again and Helen was nine. We were holding each other in the darkness of that closet and we could
hear him coming. He was calling for her. He was calling
for Helen. He found us. He found us, and he grabbed
Helen by the arm and dragged her out of the closet and
into the bedroom. I could hear her screaming, but I didn't
dare look at what he was doing to her. I closed my eyes.
I could hear her begging him to stop, but there was no
stopping him.

When he was done, Helen came back into the closet
with me. Her face was bloody and her clothes were torn.

"He was mad because my hair was short, but I was
happy because he couldn't pull it anymore."

We sat in the back of the closet together and I held Helen while she cried in my lap. I sang to her. We stayed in the closet for hours, maybe days. But Helen was never the same after that. It was like she was sick. She never wanted to get out of bed and she didn't want to play with me anymore. She just lay on the bed. Sometimes I would lie with her. I would lie beside her and tell her stories. I read books to her. She'd smile up at me and tell me she loved me.

"I know that God loves me," she'd say, "because he sent you to me. I don't know what I'd do without you, Jane."

Helen didn't hide after that. I would hide alone in the closet when Bob was drunk and when I'd come out of the closet another piece of Helen seemed to have vanished in the night. I remembered the day she died. I had skipped school. No one cared. Bob worked all day and his wife slept all day and worked all night. I was lying beside Helen in bed. She was badly beaten. I knew she was bleeding badly from some place I hadn't understood. I had wanted to call an ambulance, but she didn't want me to.

"I'm ready to go home," she'd said. "I miss my mom and dad and I know they are waiting for me. Let me die, Jane."

I had been so young. I didn't understand. All I had wanted was to make Helen happy. I had held her hand while she drew her last breath and cried when they took her body away. Social services moved me to a new foster family.

The memories faded and I looked at Helen next to me in the bed. "You're a ghost," I said. "You're dead. He killed you." I couldn't stop crying.

Helen nodded.

"You never went to heaven to see your parents?" I asked.

"I couldn't. I love you so much, Jane. I couldn't leave you alone."

"I'm so sorry, Helen. I should have helped you. I should have told someone what was happening."

"You were just six years old. Bob would have killed you if you'd told anyone. You knew that and I knew that."

I shook my head. "Thank you for staying with me."

"You're welcome."

"Do you have to go now?"

"I think it is time, but you have to know that the reason I haven't been able to see you is because there is something evil in that house. It is holding me back. It is stronger than me. It isn't a ghost. There are ghosts in Thornfield, but there is something else there, too. Something dark and evil, and it wants you, Jane. Even now, I can feel it near. You have to leave Thornfield Hall."

"I can't."

"Because of him?"

I looked down at my hands. I wanted to say it was because I had grown so fond of Miss Adele or because I loved Thornfield Hall. I did. But the truth was, I couldn't leave him.

"He's cursed. You will die if you stay with him."

"I know."

"Then leave. Leave, Jane. You have to leave before that thing gets any stronger. Because if you wait too much longer, I don't know what will happen. It wants me to leave, now. It is too strong for me."

"I can't leave Thornfield."

Helen shook her head. I lay down beside her one last time. We'd always been like sisters. She held my hand like we'd held hands in that closet all those years ago, and we slept beside each other. Morning came with its brutal light and when I awoke, she was gone. I didn't know if I would ever see her again, but I was glad she'd stayed for as long as she did. I pulled open the curtains of my bedroom window. I could never say I didn't believe in ghosts again. That meant I had to believe that whatever dark force lurked at Thornfield was real. It was real and it was evil.

# CHAPTER 10

*The night is darkening round me. The wild winds coldly blow; But a tyrant spell has bound me, and I cannot, cannot go.*

~ Emily Bronte

I VISITED MRS. BLANKENSHIP THAT morning. She sat perched at death's doorway. She had an IV in her arm and she could barely breathe. There was very little left of her. She was just a pile of bones with some skin wrapped around them. Her eyes were sunken and her lips were cracked. All that was left on her head was a few wisps of hair that the chemo hadn't taken.

"Lung cancer," she said.

It made sense. She'd smoked three packs a day since Mr. Blankenship's death.

"I'm so sorry," I said.

"No," she said. "I'm sorry. I've wronged you greatly, Jane."

"Stop that," I said. "You did everything you could for me."

"No," she said as she coughed. "No. I was a monster. It was Mr. Blankenship that wanted to adopt you and after he was gone, I abandoned you."

I put my hand on hers. Her hand felt so frail I thought I might break it. "You didn't abandon me. You let me live in your home," I asserted.

"No. I didn't. I let myself sink into a depression and I didn't protect you and nurture you the way a mother should. After you left, I got a letter from an attorney."

"What?"

"He asked if you still lived with me and I said you did. He said you had an uncle. And he was looking for you. He sent you money. Fifty thousand dollars for your college. I spent it all on myself. I was in so much debt from the medical bills…"

How could I be mad when I would have done the same for her? I was upset because she adn't told me I had an uncle. I had family. I had never had real family that I could remember. I'd assumed my parents had died of drug overdoses after they dumped me off in an ER. But, now, I had an uncle. Despite my sadness about Mrs. Blankenship's illness, it was the best news I'd heard in a very long time.

Mrs. Blankenship signaled a folded paper on her nightstand. I picked it up. It was my uncle's address and contact information. I clutched the paper to my chest.

"Thank you!" I said.

"Please forgive me…for everything?" she asked with a hacking cough.

I kissed her on the forehead. "I forgive you."

Mrs. Blankenship took a deep breath and the coughing stopped. She finally looked peaceful. I hoped Mr. Blankenship was waiting for her on the other side.

 # CHAPTER 11

*He's more myself than I am.*

~ Emily Bronte

I MADE IT BACK TO Thornfield Hall on Christmas Eve.
I had texted Mrs. Fairfax to let her know I was coming. The
house was decorated and filled with light. All the staff was
gone except for Mrs. Fairfax. She was in the kitchen cooking when I got back. The room smelled amazing. The scent
of cinnamon and cloves and butter filled the air, making
the kitchen seem alive with the spirit of the season. Mrs.
Fairfax hugged me when I came in.

"Merry Christmas," she said.

"Merry Christmas," I answered. "It looks like you're
making a feast."

"Jenna and that new boy Edward hired to take care of
the horses are off, and Edward asked me to make him a
special meal tonight. He said he wanted something roman-
tic." She raised her eyebrows at that.

I looked into Mrs. Fairfax's kind eyes and I couldn't
take it anymore. I couldn't live on the dream of some love

that would never be mine. I couldn't live in the shadows, waiting for a guy who could never be mine. Helen was right. It was time for me to leave Thornfield.

"It smells amazing," I said to Mrs. Fairfax.

I went upstairs and put my suitcase in my room. I didn't unpack it. I just left it by the door. There was no point in settling back in. I had saved enough money that I didn't really need the job anymore. I could afford to stay in the dorms. I would find a job on campus. It would be all right. I would forget Edward and Thornfield. I wasn't the first stupid girl to have her heart broken by a guy she could never have. In the grand scheme of life, it wasn't a huge deal. I would get over it. I had to.

I told myself these things, but tears burned in my eyes when I thought about leaving. The very idea of having to let go of Edward and my foolish hope made me so sad. Helen was gone forever; Mrs. Blankenship was dying; and Edward would never love me. I had an uncle, though. At least I had a relative. But at that moment, it didn't matter because my heart was breaking as I walked the halls of Thornfield looking for Edward.

I found him in the library. He was sitting by the window looking out at the snow. The wind howled through the cracks in the window. He stood up when I entered and he walked over to me. He was smiling so brightly I thought he might hug me, but instead, he just took my hand.

"Jane," he said. "I thought you might not come."

"I told you I'd be back tonight. I texted Mrs. Fairfax. I'm always true to my word."

"Of course," he said. "How could I doubt you? You never lie."

I shook my head. "I'm not Abraham Lincoln, Edward. I lie. I have flaws. Mrs. Fairfax is cooking an amazing feast. She says it's for a special dinner."

"It is," he said with a slight frown.

"I think I might go out for a while tonight. I don't want to be in the way. I would also like to turn in my notice. I have enough money to pay for the dorms now and Miss Adele really needs to be in a nursing home."

I didn't give him time to answer me. I just turned and walked, as quickly as I could, out of the room. I didn't want him to see that I was crying. I didn't want him to see the tears that were turning my cheeks splotchy and red.

Just before I made it to the front door, Edward grabbed me. He put his hand on my shoulder and stopped me from going outside.

"You're leaving?" he asked.

"I don't want to be a third wheel. You need your privacy."

"Jane, who do you think that dinner is for?"

"For you and Blanche, of course."

He laughed. He laughed at me and I felt all the tears and rage and frustration build up within me like a volcano. I couldn't take it anymore.

"What do you think I am!" I yelled. "Do you think just because I'm poor and plain and a nobody that I don't have a heart that can be broken? I am twice the woman Blanche is and I tell you, if I had half her beauty and a little money, I would have made it ten times more difficult for you to ever stop loving me than it is for me to stop loving you! Now, stop screwing with me and just let me leave."

Edward pulled me into his arms. I held him back. "Jane," he whispered. "There is a cord that goes from your heart to mine. If you ever severed it, I know I would die. I can't explain it. I feel like there is almost something supernatural binding me to you. I can't breathe when you are away."

"Stop!" I yelled. "What does that poetic crap even mean? What is this? Do you think I'm an idiot? Am I so low in your eyes that you think you can just make me the butt of all your jokes? I have never known happiness like I have known here. You've made me feel like I was important and like I mattered. You took me to the top of the world. Why would you knock me down, now? Just go to her and leave me alone! I am done with this."

"The dinner is for you, Jane. I broke up with Blanche. I told her I never cared about her and that all I have ever wanted is you. She never loved me. She only loved my money. I could barely tolerate her. I love you, Jane."

I stopped fighting him and looked up into his eyes. He was telling the truth. I could see it in his eyes, but I didn't dare believe it. Fear set in my chest like a block of ice and, even if I believed him, I couldn't accept what it might mean for me. I backed away. I could still see Bertha's ghost in my head. Loving Edward had killed Bertha. It had turned her into an angry ghost. I didn't want to be a ghost.

"You are afraid of me?" he asked. He looked wounded.

"I am," I answered plainly. "I don't want to end up like the others. I have been here long enough to believe in ghosts and curses and devils that live in attics."

"Don't be afraid…Please." His hand gently cupped my face. "My whole life, I was afraid of the curse and what it could do. I'm not afraid anymore. I love you and that makes me strong." He pulled me to him and kissed me. He kissed me with such passion and force that I thought I might melt like ice in his arms. I wrapped my arms around him and held him so tightly he could have become a part of me. I collapsed into his embrace and he lifted me off my feet. I felt so small in his arms. I felt weightless like the heat of my happiness might lift off the ground entirely and carry me away to some unknown country.

When our lips finally parted, I was breathless. I didn't care about curses. I didn't care if the Rochester men killed everyone they loved. There was something almost supernatural between us and I couldn't fight it any more than he could. Even then, part of me knew the danger that was coming, but it didn't matter. I opened my mouth to speak but there were no words that could express what I was feeling. I still couldn't believe it was real. I wanted to pinch myself to make sure I wasn't dreaming. I was crying. That was all I could do.

"Why are you crying?" he asked as he kissed my tears.

"I can't believe this is real," I said in all honesty. "I have been alone for so long."

He kissed me again. He put his hand on my cheek and kissed me. "So have I," he said. "We'll have to discover a way to let go of our loneliness, now. We can explore this new world together."

"I love you," I said in between kisses.

"Ever since I found you alone in the fog that night, I knew I could never love anyone else. You're the angel who appeared out of nowhere. You saved my life."

He kissed me again and then he put his hand in mine. I held onto it, trying to steady myself. I was light-headed and the world spun around me. I had never been kissed like this before. I had barely even been hugged. The depth and passion of his kiss made me feel like I was on a Ferris Wheel that was going too fast. I clung to him to gain my balance.

"Would you join me for dinner?" he asked as he walked me to the dining room.

"There's nothing I would like more in the world," I answered.

The dining room was spectacular. All the lights had been turned off and we dined by candlelight and Christmas light. The table was set beautifully, as though we were royalty. The meal consisted of roast turkey breast stuffed with a camembert, cashews, and cranberries, along with roasted root vegetables and crisp, finely-cut roasted sweet potatoes drizzled with a balsamic glaze. For dessert we had creamy custard tarts filled with sweet berries. It was so good. It was the best meal I'd ever had. Outside, the snow came down like a glacier was falling from Heaven. The blizzard howled and beat against the stones of Thornfield, but inside, I sat beside the roaring fire with Edward's hand in mine. I was certain I was glowing and it was my own light that was lighting the room.

After dinner we hung out in the study. Edward told me about his life in New York. He told me about how he had chosen Blanche because his grandmother had told him everything would be lost if he didn't marry someone he didn't like. He had always done what his grandmother had wanted. The entire family had, but now he thought he should have rebelled against them. He wished he had fought back and been his own person.

"I would have done as my family said forever if it weren't for you. How could I marry her, when you were here, waiting for me? I would rather lose everything than do that."

"Do you really believe in the curse?" I asked. I still wasn't entirely sure, myself. Helen had taught me that there was more on earth than could be explained by science or reason, but the curse seemed so out of this world that I wondered, if we just refused to believe it, would it cease to have power over us? Did our fear of the curse give it its power?

He smiled and kissed my hand. "I guess we'll find out soon enough."

"Maybe you can leave business school, now. You can study literature. You can live your dreams. Letting go of your family will help you. I'm glad I helped you break free."

"You bring out the best in me."

"Do I?"

"You probably don't believe this, but some people thought I was a dick before I met you."

"Really?" I raised my eyebrows. "You always seemed so friendly."

"I don't appreciate your sarcasm," he said, grinning. "I'm working on being less of a dick and I'm sure that the more time I spend with you, the easier that will be."

"Is your grandmother okay with us being together?"

"Yes, she is. She seems to think you are the answer, Jane. I think she has lost her mind. She keeps telling me that you are the door that will set us all free. I don't know. She wants me to be with you."

I nodded. "As long as she is happy."

"She is happy. She believes you are magic. I think she's right. You're here to cure us of our curse."

I laughed and we spent the rest of the evening wrapped in each other's arms. The rest of the world didn't matter. All that mattered was that I had my Edward. All the sorrow that had come before, all the ghosts and all the horror, none of it mattered because I had him and he loved me. I could weather an ocean of misfortune for one minute in his arms. He was the flame that lit my life and I wanted nothing more than to lay in his arms forever.

# CHAPTER 12

*In secret pleasure-secret tears this*
*changeful life has slipped away.*

~ Emily Bronte

WE FELL ASLEEP IN FRONT of the fire in the study. We'd stayed up so late that we just lay down together on the floor and passed out. I woke up in his arms. The fire had gone out and a cold draft pulled me from my slumber. I got up carefully. I didn't want to wake Edward. He was sleeping so peacefully. I thought, if I could find a sweater or the thermostat I could probably crawl back into his arms and fall back to sleep. I walked into the hall. Miss Adele was standing there, in the moonlight that filtered in through the window. She was wearing a thin slip. She almost appeared to be a ghost, herself. She was so thin and so pale, it was hard to even visualize her as something living.

She turned to me with a ferocity I had never known in the old woman. Her face was twisted with disgust and rage. She was like an animal. She didn't even seem human. "What did you do!!!??" she shrieked like something hell spat up. She lunged at me. For a moment, I stepped back. Fear took me and I avoided her, but she stumbled and I came to my senses.

I caught her and held onto her gently as she beat on me with her tiny little fists.

"Oh God?" she wailed. "You did this! We did this! The door is opening. HE IS COMING! THEY ARE COMING!"

I didn't know what to do. I couldn't let her go. I tried to get her back into her room, but she was so angry and I was afraid I would hurt her.

"The old ones are coming!" she yelled.

Edward emerged from the study and pulled his grand-mother from my arms. He picked her up like she was nothing more than a small child. He weathered her fists and her curses and carried her back to her bed. I made her the drugged tea while Edward held her down.

"Why? Why? Edward why? All these years! All these years and now it will all burn! Why?!" Her screams crescen-doed and became almost deafening. She broke free from Edward's embrace and began to claw at her face. "Oh God! It is horrible. It is not beautiful. I thought it would be beautiful."

I was able to give her the tea, but it was difficult. For what seemed like forever, she continued fighting and struggling and yelling about red ladies and fire. Her howls combined with the howling of the wind outside to make a cacophony that was loud enough to silence a bomb. She finally collapsed on the bed. Edward and I looked at each other with concerned alarm.

"She needs to go to a home," he said finally.

"I know," I answered.

"I always promised her I would never send her to a place like that."

"I know, but she's a danger to herself here. It's been like this, every night for a long time. What if she gets up and we don't catch her? What if she falls down the stairs or something?"

Edward nodded. "My mother never liked me very much. She always said I reminded her of my father. It was my grandmother who raised me."

"Look at her face," I whispered. I took a cloth, dampened it with some water, and gently cleaned her self-inflicted cuts.

"I should have visited her more," he whispered brokenly, "but there were so many ghosts here. So many bad things have happened in the shadows of Thornfield Hall. She wouldn't leave here and I couldn't stay."

I put my hand on his shoulder. "She's sleeping now. We should get some rest."

# CHAPTER 13

*The Shadows are as important as the light.*

~ Charlotte Bronte

IN THE MORNING, THE NURSE helped us find a place for Edward's grandmother. It was the nicest nursing home around. It was like a luxury resort, but she still wept bitterly as she was taken from Thornfield. She cried and gnashed her teeth like a woman being torn from her child. She cried out for her husband as she was taken. She cried out for him as we got her settled into her new room. There was no easy way to leave her, so the staff sedated her again.

We didn't talk much on the way back to Thornfield. The snow continued to fall. It blanketed the valley in silence. Edward and I went to a movie that night. We laughed and found a way to escape the shadows. We were happy.

Christmas break passed too quickly. It seemed like a dream to me. I felt like I was walking through the pages of a book. Every day Edward and I were together. He looked at me like I was the most special person in the world. Every moment with him was part of something I couldn't believe was real. This was not my life. This was a childhood dream of what life should be. It was like a Disney movie, where even a girl like me could grow up to be a princess. He flew me to New York and we went to the opera. He walked me through the MOMA and took me to DC to see the National Galleries and the Smithsonian. He showed me all the sights that he knew I would love because I was a dork and liked cultural stuff. He liked to tease me about that and at night he kissed me and told me he loved me. He told me I was beautiful and laughed when I blushed and protested.

"But you are beautiful," he would say. "You try to hide it behind baggy clothes, but even if you were wearing a burlap sack, you would still be the most beautiful girl I have ever seen."

Some nights our kisses would linger and his hands would run up and down my shoulders and back. A part of me wanted to go all the way. But then I'd think about him seeing my tattoo and I would pull back a little and smile shyly and tell him I wasn't ready. He always respected my boundaries. He would kiss my forehead and we would fall asleep in each other's arms. Sometimes, I would stay awake and watch the silhouette of his face in the moonlight. I would trace the curve of his lips with my fingers and study the way they parted as he slept. He was so beautiful and so perfect. I kept waiting for someone to pinch me so I could wake up from my dream.

When Edward and I returned from our trip, we went to see Miss Adele. She actually seemed better in the nursing home. She had been eating and had put on some weight. The color had returned to her cheeks and she smiled when she saw us. She still didn't make much sense when she spoke and would jump around from topic to top, speaking in snatches of conversation. Mostly, she talked about ghosts and Thornfield Hall, as well as a considerable amount of time about her bowel movements. But she seemed healthy and well cared for. She even had a gentleman friend, who smiled at her and hung around outside her room, waiting for her to join him for lunch. I was happy to know she was in a better place.

I knew that Christmas break couldn't last. I knew the dream had to die, but it didn't make it any easier when reality came bursting through my door. The weekend before I returned to classes the full-time staff returned to Thornfield Hall. The house was bustling again and the quiet solitude that had cocooned Edward and me was gone. We had to face real life, again, and we were both somewhat befuddled by it. The quiet cold of the stormy winter had left. The snow melted and the sun came out and Edward and I had to go back to school.

Mrs. Fairfax was the first one to confront me with a harsh truth. I found her in the kitchen. She was checking the food stores and I was getting a glass of juice. I smiled at her and wished her a good morning.

"What will your plans be now, Jane?" she asked kindly.

"What do you mean?" I answered.

"Miss Adele is gone and you're no longer taking care of her. We have loved having you here. You are going to need to find a new place to stay and a new source of income soon, I would imagine."

I was stunned. I hadn't even thought of that. I had been so lost in Edward, I hadn't thought about the nature of my situation.

Mrs. Fairfax's voice lowered to a whisper: "You are a wonderful girl. I'm only thinking of your best interests. I know you have something going on here with Edward and I know I'm too late to stop Edward from taking your virtue, but if you stay here receiving a paycheck and room and board, what would that make you?"

I was temporarily stunned. First of all, who said things like *taking your virtue* anymore? Secondly, I hadn't even thought of how it would look if I let Edward keep paying me when everyone was assuming I was sleeping with him. This hadn't crossed my mind. The reality of what people must be thinking of me was like a blow to the chest. "Oh," I said "No! We haven't done anything…I'll get my own place and another job once school starts. Edward and I are just dating. That's all. I'm not doing anything…Well, you know. I think he just forgot to stop the paychecks. He's my boyfriend. That's all."

Mrs. Fairfax's face went a little white. She put her hand over her mouth. "Please, don't get involved with Edward. You are such a nice girl."

"Thank you," I said. "But I can handle myself. I have been on my own for longer than you know and I am not stupid."

"Well," Mrs. Fairfax whispered, "be warned. Despite his age, Edward is a man of the world. Be careful, my dear. So many pretty girls pass through our doors. I would hate for you to be just another Blanche, cast aside when he meets another girl."

I hadn't thought of Blanche that way. She was beautiful and silly and I had never thought of her suffering heart-break on my account. I felt a little guilty. The guilt passed quickly as a new emotion pushed its way through. She said that many girls had come and gone. What if I was just one of many? What if this was just how Edward passed his time? What if the curse had left with me because he didn't actually love me, at all? My eyes filled with tears and my face flushed with anxiety.

Mrs. Fairfax put her hand on my shoulder. "Don't cry, my dear," Mrs. Fairfax said gently. "I'm sure his feelings for you are genuine. I just worry about you." She sighed deeply. "Look, I've known Edward since he was a boy. I still remember his first love. She was more beautiful than any Hollywood actress. All of his girlfriends have been stunning, but quite superficial. It was always surprising to me that Edward would be attracted to them. Even though they were beautiful, what on Earth could they talk about or have in common? But you are so different. I don't want you to be hurt like he hurt all the others. You are such a nice girl and you are so smart. Your life is only just beginning. You have so much to look forward to that has nothing to do with boys."

I smiled at Mrs. Fairfax.. I hugged her. She seemed a bit surprised, but she hugged me back. I cried on her shoulder and she just held me. She stroked my back and said, "There, there."

"You can stay on here if you like," Mrs. Fairfax said, softly. "I could find you another job around here. You could be the house historian. Edward showed me the letters you preserved. You did a wonderful job. So much of the history of this old house is rotting in the attic. We could pay you to go through the things in the attic? You will not be cast out."

I smiled. "That sounds wonderful, but you should know that I'll still be dating Edward."

"Of course, darling."

I walked away in a daze. It was bright and sunny outside and the sun streamed in through the windows, blinding me. I walked into the study and found Edward sitting on the floor reading in the dazzling sunlight. I could have just stood there watching him forever, but he looked up and smiled.

"What's wrong?" he asked when he saw my face.

"I just heard some rumors," I said.

Edward's face hardened to the scowl I had known so well in my first few months with him. "What rumors?"

"I heard that you've had a lot of girlfriends."

"My past doesn't matter."

"Am I just another girl? Will your feelings melt away when winter turns to spring?"

Edward stood up and pulled me into his arms. He was so strong and I wanted to bury myself in his arms. "I went through many girls because they were all the wrong girls. You aren't the wrong girl. You are perfect."

"What about your Bertha?"

Edward's scowl deepened. "What about her?"

80

"You loved her."

"I don't want to talk about her. All you need to know is that I love you and I will always love you."

I wanted to push and ask more questions, but I sensed I had crossed a line. I looked up at Edward. I looked up into his turbulent eyes and realized that there was a part of him he would never let me know, just like there was a part of Thornfield Hall that was hidden from me. Edward and the house were so much alike. They were haunted by old curses and dark ghosts, and both things terrified me just a little. They called to me from the darkness and I couldn't avoid them, but I was afraid of the shadows. I was afraid of the dark thing that had driven Helen away from me.

# CHAPTER 14

*The world is indeed comic, but
the joke is on mankind.*

~ H. P. Lovecraft

I WOKE UP ALONE IN Edward's bedroom. Edward was gone. The fire in the fireplace had died out and the cold darkness embraced me like a cloak. I pulled the covers up and tried to go back to sleep, but it was impossible. I turned on the bedside lamp and got up. I grabbed a sweater and threw it on over me, but the cold seeped through it like water. I wandered down the hall and into the dark, looking for Edward.

The laughter came like it always did. It surrounded me and filled me with a familiar dread. I closed my eyes. I quoted Shakespeare in my head. *By the pricking of my thumbs. Something wicked this way comes.*

I cried out for Edward. I called out with all the strength I had in my body. But there was something different about the laughter. It attacked me. It was malevolent. Suddenly, the laughter stopped and there was only quiet and darkness.

A small voice crept out of the silence like the hiss of a dying snake. "He is lying." The voice faded and I was left shivering in the dark.

Edward found me standing in the darkness, crying. He wrapped his arms around me, put a blanket over my shoulders, and walked me back to his room. I clung to his warmth. I buried my face in his chest and drank in his scent.

"Where were you?" I whispered.

I looked up at him and his face was creased with worry. "I was here," he answered. "I woke up and you were gone. I heard you crying."

I shook my head. "No," I said. "You were gone. I woke up and you were gone. I was alone."

"Where would I have gone?" he asked. "I never left the bed. I was always here. You must have been dreaming. Maybe you were sleepwalking?"

He tucked me into bed and climbed in beside me. He held me close. I could hear the gentle thump of his heart through his shirt. Outside the window, the wind whispered. The moon cast strange shadows on Edward's face.

"Are you all right?" he asked.

I nodded, but I wasn't all right. I was afraid. For the first time since I had entered Thornfield Hall, I began to feel the true nature of the darkness that lived in the shadows of this place that I loved most in the world. I felt death and horror and decay so old that the very bricks of Thornfield were young by comparison. And I knew the darkness was telling me the truth when it said that Edward was lying.

# CHAPTER 15

*For even in the greatest of
horrors irony is seldom absent.*

~ H.P. Lovecraft

MY SECOND-SEMESTER CLASS LOAD PROVED
to be even more daunting than my first. Physics and
Microbiology, alone, were enough to turn my hair gray, but
add Vertebrate Reproduction and Human Physiology to
the mix and I knew I probably wouldn't be sleeping much.
My medical mission group met that evening and Sinjun
and the girls were all a-flutter. Our mission had gotten a
grant, which meant we had full funding to go to Haiti and
work all summer.

"This is my last summer before I start med school,"
Sinjun said with a huge smile. "This will be perfect. I get
one last trip before I'm drowning."

Mary laughed. "It is completely sad that spending
the summer helping the poverty-stricken Haitians with
medical care is your idea of a vacation before medical
school."

Sinjun rolled his eyes at Mary. "What are you doing for your last summer?"

"Next summer, after I graduate, I'm going to the Bahamas. I'm going to work on my tan and find the love of my life, or at least a fun fling."

Sara smiled. "I'm with you. Haiti is not where I'm spending my last summer before medical school. You're hardcore, Sinjun. Nothing but work and good deeds for you. Have you ever even had a real vacation?"

"Of course I have. My parents took me to Disney World when I was ten," he said.

Mary laughed again. "Really. That was your last vacation?"

"I went to Interlochen summer art camp, three years in a row, to perfect my violin. I had a great time."

"You're a lost cause," Sara said with an impish grin. "Help us out here, Jane. Tell Sinjun he's lost. What are you doing with your last summer before medical school?"

"I'm only a Freshman. I haven't even thought that far ahead, yet."

"So, what was your last vacation?" she asked.

"My boyfriend took me to New York to see the opera over Christmas break."

Mary jumped up. "Are you kidding me?" she exclaimed. "You have a boyfriend? Why haven't I heard about this? Who are you dating?"

"His name is Edward Rochester."

"Holy Shit on a Cracker," Sara said. "Are you kidding me? Can you pay for my medical school? I'm looking for a wealthy benefactor."

Mary hit Sara on the arm. "Don't be rude. She can't help you because she's helping me."

I looked over at Sinjun. He seemed to be frowning. "I didn't know you had a boyfriend," he said suddenly.

I didn't answer him. The question seemed loaded and I wasn't sure what the proper response was. He picked up a stack of papers. "We should get back to work. We'll need to make sure we get all our shots before we go. Jane, do you think you could look into getting more donations for eyeglasses? There's always a big need for glasses on these types of trips."

"Sure thing," I said.

He turned back to his work and I went back to mine. Sara and Mary laughed and chatted on about their perfect dream vacations. They teased me about my rich fiancé and asked me if I would pay for their vacations. It seemed like any other meeting we might have, but Sinjun was quiet and I felt that quiet like a wall between us.

I made it back to Thornfield late. All the staff was gone and the house was shrouded in silence. I wandered around until I found Edward tucked away in his study surrounded by papers. I had never seen Edward work before. I tiptoed into the room and set my books down quietly on a table in the back of the room. He didn't seem to notice me. I walked up behind him and kissed him.

"What are you doing?" I asked quietly.

"I'm working," he growled.

"What on?" I asked.

"Homework. I have to go back to school soon. I hate to leave you, but I'm falling behind."

I hadn't thought about Edward's classes. He'd seemed so laid back about school, it was easy to forget he was at Yale. He seemed anxious and stressed, so I curled up in the big chair in front of the fireplace and lost myself in my own work. It was easy to forget about Edward's moods when I had so much studying to do.

After an hour or so, Edward got up and stretched. The fire was beginning to sputter out and Edward threw another log into the flames. The fire crackled and hissed. Sparks spat out of the darkness. I stared into the flames and watched Edward blow on the fire until it glowed. Warmth filled the room, but I shivered.

"We're collecting glasses for a medical mission," I said as I stared into the flames. "Would you like to donate any?"

Edward walked to his desk and wrote a check. He handed it to me and sat down beside me. The check was made out to cash and it was for $100,000. I couldn't breathe. I had never held a check with so many zeroes.

"This can definitely buy a lot of glasses," I said. "It's too much, Edward."

He shrugged dismissively. "I'm sure you can find something the medical mission can use the money for."

Edward leaned over and kissed me. I wrapped my arms around him and pulled him to me. He took my face in his hands and kissed my forehead and then my lips. He let his hands slide down my arms as he kissed my neck. I sighed. "She walks in beauty like the night," he said as his hands slid down around my waist.

"Don't," I said softly. "Don't call me beautiful. Don't pretend I'm a Blanche. I'm just Jane. I will never walk in beauty like the night. Poets will never write sonnets for me."

Edward pushed a stray lock of hair out of my face. "What happened to you when you were young that you are so terrified of being beautiful, of standing out? You *are* beautiful. I can't pretend you aren't and, no matter how much you hide yourself behind your hair or baggy clothes, your beauty shines through. Who hurt you so much that you can't let anyone see the beauty in you?"

I flushed and closed my eyes. I tried to hold back my tears. I could still see Helen in my mind's eye. I could hear her telling me to cut her pretty hair. I could hear her screams. I wished she was still with me. I missed her so much it hurt. I missed her lovely face and good heart.

Edward kissed my tears away, "Tell me."

"When I was very young, I was in foster care. I had a foster sister and I loved her like she was my own sister. Every night our foster father came for her because she was so beautiful. I had to watch and listen to what he did to her, but he never came for me because I wasn't beautiful. I was safe because I was ugly."

Edward pulled me to him and I wrapped my arms around him and sobbed into his shirt as he stroked my hair.

"Men like that don't hurt little girls because they are beautiful," he said. "They hurt little girls because they can. They are evil. It wasn't your ugliness that saved you. It was your strength. You are a survivor and you are beautiful. Never forget that."

I reached up and touched his face. He knew everything about me. I was stripped bare before him, but I didn't know him. "Why can't you tell me what you're hiding from?" I asked him.

He looked away from me, into the roaring fire. "Oh Jane," he said. "I wish I could tell you everything."

"Trust me," I said. "I love you."

He smiled down at me and kissed my forehead. "I have to leave tomorrow. Do you think you'll be all right, in the house, by yourself?"

"I'll be fine. I have so much work to do I probably won't be here that much as it is. I'm sure I'll be living at the library at Huntington until the end of semester."

"Sweet Jane," he whispered. "Don't ever change."

Edward kissed me again. His hands slid up under my shirt and I jumped backward. So far, I had been able to hide the thing that was on my back, but I knew the closer Edward and I got, the harder it would be to avoid him seeing my body. Edward misinterpreted my reaction.

"I'm sorry. I didn't mean to make you feel pressured. I don't want you to ever feel like you have to do anything you aren't ready for. I can wait forever if I have to."

I smiled and kissed Edward. "Thank you."

I guess I was still keeping secrets too.

# CHAPTER 16

*There are horrors beyond life's edge that we
do not suspect, and once in a while man's
evil prying calls them just within our range.*

~ H.P. Lovecraft

I MISSED EDWARD TERRIBLY WHILE he was
away. I missed his arms around me at night. Thornfield
Hall seemed all the more haunted when he wasn't in it.
The laughter tormented me and I spent most of the week
falling asleep in the library. I did everything I could to
avoid Thornfield's ghosts. I even invited myself to a party
at Mary's apartment. Mary, Sara, and Sinjun all shared a
huge apartment, just off campus. They all split the rent.
It wasn't really an apartment, more of an old Victorian
mansion that had been cut up into apartments. They had
the first floor.

The party was small and intimate and it made it much
harder for me to hide in the corner. Mary and Sara kept
introducing me to everyone. Almost everyone there was
pre-med and I found myself drawn into conversations about

MCATs and medical schools and what people wanted to specialize in. I even had a small glass of wine. I found myself laughing and opening up. It wasn't like a high school party where everybody split off into cliques. It wasn't like Edward's party, filled with beautiful people. Everyone at the party was like me. They had interests. I didn't feel like a weirdo or a freak. Everybody wanted to talk to me and include me.

Sara got quite drunk by the end of the night and she and her boyfriend, Billy, sat curled up on the couch. Her boyfriend was a senior and an art major. He seemed to be Sara's opposite. He was a bit of a hippie, but the two of them seemed happy.

"I heard you live at Thornfield Hall," Billy said to me.

"I do," I answered. My cheeks were flushed from wine and attention. The room grew quiet and all eyes fell on me.

"Is it true?" Billy asked. "Is Thornfield haunted? I heard that the Rochester men keep the bodies of their dead wives in the basement."

"I think the house would smell bad if there were that many corpses rotting in the basement," I said, trying to make light of where the conversation was headed.

"But is the house haunted?" Mary asked.

I looked into my glass of wine. I didn't want to admit that I had seen ghosts, but the wine loosened my tongue. "It is," I answered.

"What have you seen?" a guy in the back of the room asked. "Do the Rochester men murder their wives?"

"No!" I laughed. "I started working there to take care of one of the Rochester wives, who is in her 90s. She outlived her husband."

"What's Edward Rochester like?" Sara asked. "I heard he gets around."

"Maybe he used to be, but he's always been a gentleman with me. He's..." I couldn't find the words to describe Edward. They eluded me and I found myself blushing and stammering.

Mary giggled. "You've got it bad, don't you? I can see why. He's gorgeous and filthy-stinking rich."

I shook my head. "He's more than that."

"What about ghosts?" Sinjun asked.

"I've only seen two," I said. "One is dressed in white and she wanders the halls at night. She's not scary, she's very sweet. The other is a girl, all in red, and she scares me." I paused. My breath caught in my throat. "There is something else there, too."

"Something else?" Mary asked. She leaned forward, hungry for more information.

I'd been drinking and my tongue was looser than it should have been, so I continued when I knew I should have stopped talking. "There is some old evil there. There is a curse. Sometimes, it's terrifying to be there alone. There are so many ghosts that the house feels more alive at night than during the day."

"You see," Billy said. "They're the ghosts of the murdered Rochester wives."

"I heard that it was haunted by the ghost of a maid who killed herself when one of the Rochester men left her broken-hearted," a girl from the back shouted out.

Sinjun picked up his glass of ginger ale and retreated to his room. I left everybody to discuss which ghost haunted Thornfield to follow him.

"Have I done something wrong?" I asked him.

"No, Jane, not at all," he answered. "I just have a headache."

"I got the donations for the glasses." I handed him Edward's check.

He turned a little pale when he saw it. "You've got to be kidding me?"

"What?" I asked.

"Edward Rochester just gave us $100,000 for the mission? Just like that?"

"He's very generous."

"Shit. That's more than the actual grant." Sinjun shook his head and put the money on his desk. He sat down on his bed. "I really need to get some sleep. Do you mind, Jane?"

I left Sinjun to his headache and went back out into the party. Everyone was beginning to leave. It was very late and almost everybody was drunk.

"You should stay, Jane," Mary said.

"I should?"

"Yeah. You look like you've had quite a bit to drink and it's a long walk home in the dark. You can stay in the guest room. I'll get you some PJs to sleep in."

I took the pajamas and collapsed into the bed. It was nice to sleep someplace that wasn't tormented by ghosts. I slept better than I had in months. I awoke to sunshine bathing me in warmth. It drifted in through the lace curtains and filled the room with light. I stretched and yawned. I felt completely rested for the first time in as long as I could remember. It didn't take me long to climb out of the comfortable bed and clean myself up. I got dressed and tied my hair back into a neat ponytail. I washed my face and put on a little lip gloss and emerged to a very messy apartment.

Beer bottles, empty plastic cups and paper plates with remnants of pizza crust were scattered all over. I tiptoed around the mess and made my way into the kitchen. The apartment was quiet. Everyone else had had a lot to drink, and I assumed they were still sleeping off their hangovers. I knew how to be quiet around drunk people. Living with Mrs. Blankenship had taught me that. I didn't expect to find anyone awake. I snuck into the kitchen to make coffee in hopes that I could leave before everyone woke up from their drunken cocoons. I wasn't lucky enough to get my wish, however. I had forgotten that Sinjun hadn't had anything to drink.

Sinjun was sitting at the breakfast table with a massive book on Physiology spread out in front of him. The coffee was already brewed and Sinjun had a cup larger than his head. I poured myself a mug and sat down across from him. He stopped reading and looked at me intensely.

"Are you really living with that jerk?" he blurted out. "You are way too young to be living with a guy."

I took a sip of the coffee and stared into the blackness of the bitter brew. "He's not a jerk," I said. "He's wonderful and I'll be seventeen in March."

"I don't think you know him as well as you think you do. You are too young to live with anyone and you've only known this guy for less than a year. What do your parents think about this?"

"I don't have parents."

Sinjun shifted uncomfortably and looked back at his book. "I'm sorry. It's none of my business. I just think you're really smart and you are going to be an amazing doctor. I would just hate to think that some guy would get in the way of that."

I blushed. "Thank you," I said. "It means a lot that you think so highly of me. You're a good friend and I don't have many friends. It's nice to have someone who worries about me."

Sinjun cracked a smile. He put his hand on mine. "Of course, I worry about you." His face was usually so serious, but when he smiled his eyes lit up.

"I promise I won't let my living arrangements get in the way of my studies. Edward is a good guy. I get free room and board at Thornfield and I'm going to be working part-time organizing and preserving the old documents and artifacts in the attic since Miss Adele is in a nursing home now."

Sinjun's smile faded. He shook his head and looked back at the pages of his book. His hand left mine. "That guy has a rep. Just be careful," he warned. "You're only sixteen."

"Of course, I'll be careful. I may be young but I'm an old soul," I answered firmly. "Where have you decided to go for med school?" I asked, changing the subject. "You got into five schools, right?"

He shifted and looked at me again. "I'm going to Vanderbilt. It's a good school and it isn't too far from home for me."

"I got a scholarship to Vanderbilt, but I decided to come here instead when I found the job at Thornfield. Besides, I'm not a fan of country music."

"It's not like everyone who lives in Nashville likes country music. I hate country music and my family's from the South."

"I never would have thought so. Where's your accent?"

"We're from Atlanta. We don't have accents," he said with a wink.

"Do you need help cleaning up?"

Sinjun looked out at the mess around him. It was like he was just noticing it. He seemed like the type of guy that wouldn't notice a spider if it was crawling up his nose. He just focused on the work in front of him and ignored everything else.

Sinjun shook his head. "Don't worry about it. The girls will clean it up. They make the messes. They clean them up."

"I guess I'll see you tomorrow at the meeting?" I said as I stood to leave.

Sinjun grunted in agreement and returned to his work. I couldn't bring myself to leave without helping a little, so I cleaned up the living room, tossing out the cups and paper plates and lining up the empty beer bottles on the counter. The place was still pretty messy, but I had at least cleaned up most of the party garbage before I left.

# CHAPTER 17

*At night, when the objective world
has slunk back into its cavern and
left dreamers to their own, there com
inspirations and capabilities impossible
at an less magical and quiet hour.*

~ H.P. Lovecraft

EDWARD CAME BACK ON SATURDAY. I hadn't realized how much I had missed him until he found me in the library. He sat down beside me and put a carefully wrapped box in front of me. He was smiling. He seemed so pleased with himself. He looked more laid back than usual. He was wearing jeans and a t-shirt that showed off his biceps. He looked like he had gotten a little sun. His skin was bronzed.

"You must have had a few good weeks," I commented from over my Physics book.

"I tied up a lot of loose ends," he said with a devilish grin.

"You look awfully sun-bronzed for someone who's been in class for the last month," I said.

He pushed the gift toward me. "Open it."

"You don't have to buy me things."

"I don't have to, but I want to. Would you open it?"

I took the gift reluctantly and carefully peeled the gold paper from the box. Beneath the paper, there was a brown box labeled Kindle. I opened the box and saw the newest edition of the most popular e-reader on the market. It was shiny and new and said it had 4-G and Wi-Fi and all the other bells and whistles. I held the sleek back device in my hands. It felt wrong. I loved the smell of old books and paper. I loved the way the pages of a book sounded when they turned. This electronic device felt like it would slowly suck the joy from the pages of the books.

"Do you love it?" he asked. "I know you don't like jewelry or clothes, but I thought that this would be perfect. I put an ungodly amount of money on your account so you can have any book you want anytime you want it. You literally have the entire library at your fingertips. The best part is that you can download your textbooks, so you won't have to drag those enormous books around with you everyplace. You can just take this and a few notebooks with you to class and you are set."

He seemed so pleased with himself. I couldn't bring myself to say anything negative about his gift. I smiled and kissed him. "I love it," I said.

He took it from me and fiddled with it. "I already downloaded all your textbooks." He handed it back to me. The screen had the exact page from the book I was reading on it. It did seem kind of amazing.

"Thank you," I whispered.

Edward pulled me into his arms and kissed me so hard I felt my breath leave my body with him. I put my hand on his arm and slid it up his bicep and under his shirt. I ran my fingers over the tight sinews of his chest. He drew a deep breath and let his hands slide down my back. He slowly eased me down to the floor and lay on top of me. He lifted the bottom of my shirt and ran his hands over my naked skin as he kissed my neck. I gasped for breath. I wanted him so badly, I knew that all he would have to do was ask and I would be his, but he stopped. He sat up and looked down at me. I reached out to him, but he shook his head.

"I want to do this right," he said. "Jane, there have been a lot of other girls. I don't want to lie to you, but I don't want you to be one of them. I want to wait until I know you are ready."

I sat up and pulled my shirt back down. I had become so lost in the moment, I had forgotten about the one thing I was afraid of him seeing. I had forgotten to keep my tattoo hidden. He hadn't noticed, but I had to be careful. I couldn't lose myself, again.

We lay back down and relaxed, again. I studied him, lying next to me with his shirt off. He wasn't gym-toned, but he was perfect to me. He was lean and beautiful. He had a long scar along his rib cage. It was jagged and angry. It wasn't his only scar and, as I studied him, I noticed something I had never seen before. Partially hidden by the waistband of his pants, on his back, was a network of small scars that almost looked like pieces of cracked egg-shell. I reached out and touched them and Edward jumped.

"What are they?" I asked softly.

Edward pulled his shirt back on and shook his head. "They're crazy."

"What?"

"You'll think I'm insane."

"I wouldn't care if you were mentally ill. I would love you all the same. Mental illness is treatable."

Edward kissed me. "My family always said that we would shatter and turn back to dirt, eventually. My father said I was hollow inside and that I would die soulless and alone. My father told me that these were the cracks. Since I have been with you, they have been getting smaller. They're almost gone now."

"You should go to a doctor. They could be a sign of a disease and your family's crazy superstition has kept you from getting proper treatment." I was a fine one to talk; me and my growing tattoo.

"I have. The doctor didn't have a clue. He said it must be a rash."

I shook my head and studied the cracks. Maybe he was dirt. Maybe I was the devil. Maybe we were all cursed and I would die soon and he would turn to dust. I felt like I was losing my mind.

That night we went to bed early. It was hard to lay in his arms and not do anything else. It was hard to kiss him and not go much further. I wanted to be one with him, and as I drifted off to sleep I found myself dreaming of things good girls aren't supposed to dream about. Just as my dream was about to get really racy, the scent of smoke lifted me from my fantasy. It pulled me out of my slumber and called to me. I sat up. Edward was still asleep. He could sleep through anything. I sniffed the air. I got up and followed the smell down the hall until the smoke was so thick and black that it burnt my eyes and stung my nose.

"Edward!" I cried out.

The smoke was billowing out of my bedroom. I ran to my room and screamed. I screamed so loudly it would even wake Edward from his sleep. Inside my room, my bed was on fire and words were carved into the floor. The words were written in a language I couldn't understand, but I could read the words next to them. *Don't open the door*, was written in ash in front of my bed. I coughed and covered my nose and mouth with my hands. I felt the smoke burn in my lungs. I grabbed my laptop off my desk and hugged it to me. My eyes were drowning in tears and my vision became so blurry I couldn't see my way forward.

I turned away from my burning bed and saw her standing in the doorway. She blocked my escape. The flames spread rapidly, filling the room with black smoke. The red lady stood in front of me, cackling like a wicked witch in some fairy tale. Her red dress was on fire. The heat from the fire around me burnt my eyes, but there was no way out. She was going to kill me. Bertha, the red lady, Edward's first girlfriend, was going to kill me.

"You can't be here," Bertha said in a hiss. "You can't be with him. The door will open and bleed. You know the truth, Jane. You know what sleeps beneath your flesh. I will see you burn before I see you wake it. You need to leave." Bertha laughed hysterically for a minute and then she walked toward me. "Can't you see it yet? Can't you see what you are doing? Stupid girl!"

Bertha laughed one last time and then vanished. In a kind of blind desperation, I backed away from where she'd been standing. I turned and ran blindly. I had no idea where I was running. I couldn't see because of the smoke and I smacked into the wall. The force of it knocked me off my feet and I fell to the floor. Everything went black and I was swallowed up by darkness and pain. The last thing I remembered hearing was a horrible, bell-like laughter that drifted up through the smoke like it was made of fire.

When I woke up again, I was lying in Edward's bed. I was wearing one of Edward's shirts and my head was bandaged. My head throbbed like someone had used my face as a percussion instrument in a band. It was daylight, but the curtains were drawn.

I tried to sit up, but the pain in my head was too overwhelming and I lay back down immediately. I wanted to cry, my head hurt so badly. The night before was like a smoky haze. The only thing I could remember clearly was the sight of Bertha in her burning red dress, laughing at me. I opened my eyes. Edward was sitting beside my bed. He had fallen asleep. A book was lying open on his chest, as if he had passed out and while reading. His hair was disheveled and he had enough stubble on his cheek to look as if he were trying to grow a beard. He wore nothing but a t-shirt and some old jeans. He almost didn't look like himself.

Edward sat up when he realized I was awake. The book fell off his chest and onto the floor. He grabbed my hands and kissed them. "Thank God," he said. He covered my face with kisses. I couldn't help but smile. Edward's passion was like a wave I couldn't help being carried away by.

I became aware of pain. My arms hurt and my stomach felt like the skin had been peeled off and replaced with duct tape. I moaned in agony.

"Nurse!" Edward bellowed. "She's in pain."

The nurse came in with a needle and put something in my arm. I squealed as the needle punctured my skin and Edward kissed my forehead. He whispered sweetly into my ear and promised me that the pain would be gone. He didn't lie. The nurse left and a sweet oblivion washed over me. It was like I was being carried away on a fluffy white cloud. I sunk into my pillow and looked up at Edward.

"I love you," I said.

"I love you, too," he answered.

"She came again, didn't she," I whispered. "She came with fire. She'll never leave you."

"Who?"

"Bertha."

Edward drew back. His face turned to stone. "What do you know about Bertha?"

"I know she's haunting you. I know she won't rest until we both burn." I laughed. I felt like my head was a bubble. I was floating above my body instead of sitting in it.

Whatever that nurse had given me was strong. "Everyone who matters in my life is a ghost. I'm surrounded by lost phantoms, waiting for me in the fog. Are you even real?"

"You're talking nonsense," he answered. "It's the morphine. There are no ghosts here.. There is only you and me."

I laughed again. "Maybe we're the ghosts. Maybe we just don't know it yet."

Edward leaned forward. "Go to sleep. Your burns are healing. You'll be well soon."

"Did you see it?" I asked as I realized I was in different clothing. He must have changed me.

"Did I see what?" he asked.

"Did you see the door?"

"I saw enough to get you out."

I drifted off to sleep, knowing Edward still didn't know my secret, but when I looked down at my arms, I could see that I wouldn't be able to hide my marks much longer. I was evolving. I dreamt of fire and ghosts. I was walking through an endless fog. Those who had left me rose up from the fog to greet me. My mother and father were there in the fog. They reached out for me. They called my name, but I could not touch them. They were as insubstantial as the fog that surrounded them. Helen stood beside them. She was weeping. She didn't look up at me. And then she walked away. I turned and found myself face to face with the two ladies of Thornfield Hall. The two phantoms guarded a great golden doorway. The white lady stood to the right of the door and she held a bird in a silver cage. The red lady held a dragon in her arms. The dragon puffed smoke and growled.

"You can never open the door!" the red lady snarled.

I sat up. My pain was gone. I wasn't sure how much time had passed. I think I may have drifted in and out of consciousness. I remembered, only vaguely, what had happened. I remembered Edward. I remembered nurses with pills and needles. I had a catheter in. I struggled in my bed. Edward looked up from his book.

"Are you hurting?" he asked.

I shook my head. "I just feel groggy," I answered. "What happened?"

"You ran into the fire. I didn't get to you on time. You were burnt, but not too badly. You had a lot of smoke inhalation injury. It damaged your esophagus and trachea. You were in a lot of pain, so we've kept you pretty doped up."

"H-How long was I out for?"

"About three days. You missed two days of school."

"Crap," I muttered. "I had a test."

"What were you thinking?" Edward asked. "Why the hell would you run into that fire? You could've died?"

"I tried to save my laptop," I grumbled. "Did it get destroyed in the fire?"

"I'll buy you a new laptop." He shook his head. "You never have to worry about material things ever again." He leaned down and kissed my lips. "Promise me you won't be foolish like that, again."

"I promise." I gave him a wobbly smile and he touched my face. I noticed his arms. They were covered in bandages. "What happened to your arms?"

"I got burned carrying you out of the fire."

"I'm sorry you got hurt. I-I didn't know it was such a big fire."

"Why didn't you run when you realized how big it was?"

I shook my head. "I can't remember," I lied.

Edward sighed. "Are you feeling well enough to get up? The doctor said you should do some walking when you woke up."

I nodded and Edward got the nurse. I spent the day slowly walking the halls of Thornfield with Edward. He held me up while I regained my strength. My burns weren't as bad as I'd thought. Most of the damage done was from the smoke. That night I fell asleep in Edward's bandaged arms. I felt so safe there. I never wanted to leave. I wanted to drown in his embrace.

It was a week before I could go back to school, but I made it back. Time passed quickly. I had so much work and Edward had to go back to school, too. My room was repaired. It was as if nothing had happened. All evidence of the fire was erased, and Edward and I spent more and more of our time on the weekend locked in each other's arms. We were moving too fast. We both knew it.

# CHAPTER 18

*That is not Dead which can eternal lie and
with strange eons even death may die.*

~ H.P. Lovecraft

EDWARD SUGGESTED WE GET AWAY for
Spring Break. The Rochester Group owned a lot of property, including a condo complex in Naples, Florida, and
Edward had access to the penthouse whenever he wanted.
The night before we left, I had my bags packed and I was
trying to figure out how I was going to tell Edward about
my tattoos. It was time and there was no way I could go to
the sunshine state without revealing my secret.

The next day dawned cool but sunny. It was a bit chilly,
but not so cold it was uncomfortable. The scent of spring
flowers drifted through the air. I woke up early and went
into town to get my hair and makeup done. I'd even bought
a pretty blue sundress, with a matching blue knit sweater,
to wear on the plane.

"You look lovely," Mrs. Fairfax said softly in the doorway of my room. There was a sadness in her voice.

I looked in the mirror. My hair fell in soft layers around my face and down over my shoulders. The hairdresser had cut it so that it framed my face instead of hiding it. And the makeup they applied at the salon wasn't over-done or dramatic. My lips were red and full, my cheekbones had a glow. They even plucked my eyebrows so that they gave my eyes a more dramatic look. My eyes seemed large and dark in my rounded face. I had put on a few pounds since starting college. What they called the 'freshman fifteen.' It was more like the 'sneaky seven' for me. But given that I was so skinny to begin with, the weight gain suited me. I had always been so poor that food was a luxury, and now I actually had curves where before there were only angles. I felt beautiful inside and out and, for the first time in my life, I wasn't afraid of that. I was proud of the beauty I had suddenly blossomed into. I wasn't hiding behind my long hair or under bulky old sweatshirts and baggy jeans. I smiled into the mirror. I buttoned the sweater that was keeping my tattoo covered. It was time to tell the full truth…for both of us.

"Are you ready?" Mrs. Fairfax asked.

I nodded. Butterflies fluttered about in my stomach. Mrs. Fairfax took off a blue topaz ring she was wearing and put it on my finger. I looked down at it. It wasn't anything extravagant. It was simple and small, but it was pretty and made my finger sparkle.

"What's this for?" I asked.

"It's a gift," Mrs. Fairfax replied.

"You don't need to do that," I protested.

"I care about you, Jane," Mrs. Fairfax said. "Just take the gift."

I gave Mrs. Fairfax a big hug. She embraced me tightly and kissed my cheek. "You're in my prayers."

I carried my suitcase downstairs to wait for Edward. I planned on telling him about my curse after we got settled on the plane. I knew he would understand. I had understood all of his scars and ghosts. He would have to understand mine.

Edward greeted me with a smile. He was dressed casually in shorts and a t-shirt. I liked him best that way. I liked him looking comfortable. He looked more like a boy and less like an angry man. He kissed me.

"Are you ready?" he asked.

I smiled as I opened my mouth to say yes, but the words didn't come out. The words were cut short by the front doors opening. I recognized the guy that came barreling in immediately. It was the young man who had been hurt a few weeks ago. He burst in and came running into the foyer. Edward stepped forward, putting me behind him, as though he wanted to protect me.

"I got you, you bastard!" the man yelled at Edward. "You killed my sister, Bertha!"

I reached out for Edward's hand and gripped it so tightly my knuckles went white. This wasn't happening. This couldn't be happening. It wasn't possible.

The door swung open again and two police officers in uniform and one in plain clothes followed. The plainclothes officer put his hand on Edward's shoulder.

"Edward Rochester?" he asked.

"Yes," Edward answered.

"You are under arrest for the murder of Bertha Mason."

The officer was reading Edward his Rights. He had the right to remain silent. If he gave up this right anything he said would be held against him in a court of law...

Edward turned to me and grabbed me with his one free hand. He pulled me to him and held me so close I could have been fused to his side.

"You've made a mistake," I said in a panic. "Bertha killed herself. She jumped from the tower."

"No," Bertha's brother spat out. "I finally did what I should have done for my sister all those years ago. I had her exhumed and ordered an autopsy. She'd been stabbed three times before she fell from that tower. You murdered my sister, you bastard!

I let go of Edward's hand.

"Please," Edward pleaded. "Jane, you have to understand. This isn't what you think. She was crazy. She was a drug addict. Please, Jane!"

"Did you stab her Edward?" I asked.

"Yes, but I can explain." He wrestled himself free of the officers and pulled up his shirt with his one free hand. There was a hideous scar running down his left side. I had seen it before, but I had assumed it was part of the cracks on his skin that he'd told me about. "She tried to kill me. She did this. I had no choice."

I backed away from Edward. There had never been a curse. He was a murderer. It all made sense, now. It made more sense than some stupid curse. He had killed Bertha. Maybe his father had killed his mother, too. All the rumors were true and the only ghosts haunting Thornfield were the ghosts of murdered women.

"You had to stab her three times and set her on fire?" the brother yelled. "She had burns all over her. It looked like someone had put cigarettes out on her."

I closed my eyes. I could still see the phantom red lady burning in my room. I could smell the smoke that had burnt my lungs.

"I didn't burn her and I didn't push her!" Edward protested.

The officer wrestled Edward to the ground and put the handcuffs on him. "You have the right to an attorney. If you can't afford one, one will be provided for you..."

I turned and walked away from him. I could hear Edward calling my name. He was screaming for me, but he was a murderer who had stabbed his first girlfriend three times, set her on fire, and then threw her from the tower. How could I love a man who was capable of such evil? *He had set her on fire.* I walked out of the house and through the gardens that were still bright with spring flowers. The birds still sang and the breeze still carried the scent of cherry blossoms, but it all seemed bitter. The evil in the house had been Edward. It had always been Edward. Everyone had warned me. Helen, Mrs. Fairfax, Jenna. Everyone had warned me.

I went up to my room and stripped off my pretty new dress. I washed the makeup from my face and tied my hair back in a ponytail. I put on my old jeans and my favorite Gryffindor t-shirt. I packed everything I owned into the suitcase I had come with. I climbed into my old Jeep and drove away.

# CHAPTER 19

*Uncertainty and danger are always closely allied, thus making any kind of an unknown world as a world of peril and evil possibilities.*

~ H.P. Lovecraft

I DIDN'T HAVE ANY PLACE to go, so for a while, I just sat in the parking lot of a McDonalds and sobbed. I leaned against my steering wheel and cried until my eyes didn't have any tears left. Part of me thought that, if I sat in that parking lot long enough, something would happen. Edward would come knock on the window and tell me the police had learned it was all a terrible mistake. Bertha had killed herself. I thought that some miracle would happen and everything would be all right. I thought, maybe I would wake up in Edward's arms and everything that had happened would have been a terrible dream.

As the sun began to set, I realized I would have to leave my Jeep. I would have to go the ATM and take out my hard-earned money. I would find someplace to spend the night. I couldn't just sit in my car sobbing for the rest of my life. I wiped the tears from my cheeks and laughed at myself. How ridiculous to think that I could live happily ever after. I had never had anything given to me in my life. Everything I had, I'd worked for, far harder than I should have had to. Girls like me didn't get to fall in love with passionate, brilliant, beautiful men, who were too good to be true. I was such a fool. There was no such thing as fairy tales and I had been deluding myself into thinking I had found one. There were no Prince Charmings. I'd grown up in a world with too many bad guys, who did bad things to girls and women. I should have known better.

Just as I was blowing my nose, Mary knocked on the window of my Jeep. I rolled it down and looked up at her.

"Are you okay?" she asked.

I wanted to lie. I wanted to dry my tears and tell her I was fine, but I choked on the words before they even left my lips and I began to cry again.

Mary ran around to the other side of the car and got in. She grabbed hold of me and hugged me. For a long time, I just cried on her shoulder. I cried until I didn't have any tears left to cry.

"What happened?"

I shook my head. "He wasn't who I thought he was," I blubbered. "It was all a lie and now I don't have any place to go. I don't know what to do."

"That's stupid," Mary said, as she released me from her iron hug. She wiped the tears from my face with her sleeve and pushed my hair behind my ear. My curly hair had rebelled against the pony tail holder and was a mess again. Mary tried to fix it but it was like fighting the rain with your hands. "You do have someplace to go. You are coming to stay with us. You always have a place with us."

I wiped my nose on the back of my hand. "Really?"

"Of course," she said. "You are one of our best friends." She giggled. "And I'm positive you're going to be super successful and very important someday, so I want to start kissing up to you now."

I laughed in spite of everything

"Let's go home," Mary said. "I walked here and if I hadn't seen you bawling in your Jeep, I would have had to do the healthy thing and walk home, and that goes against everything my fast-food diet stands for. You don't know it, but you're the one who saved me." Mary smiled and I turned the key in the ignition and drove us back to the apartment. I carried my heavy suitcase up the stairs and Mary cleaned up the guest bedroom for me. She even found clean sheets for me. It wasn't a big room, but it was cozy and safe. There wouldn't be any crazy cackling in the middle of the night, or ghosts appearing in front of me and telling me secrets, or any fires threatening my life. And most importantly, there would be no one to break my heart.

"How much is rent?" I asked.

"Don't worry about rent," Mary said.

"Really," I said. "I have money saved up. How much is it?"

"How about $100 a month. Is that okay?"

"Yeah, that's great," I said.

Sara suddenly came bursting through the front door. She didn't look around. She just tossed her books on the sofa. She was talking before the door even shut behind her.

"Oh my God!" she exclaimed. "Did you hear the news? Edward Rochester really did kill his old girlfriend."

"Sara," Mary said angrily.

"Do you think Jane knows?"

"Sara," Mary said again.

"They say he stabbed her, set her on fire, and pushed her out a window. What a psycho! I hope Jane's okay. That poor girl. She was only sixteen when he killed her. He obviously gets them young and vulnerable…"

"Sara!" Mary yelled.

Sara finally stopped talking and turned to face Mary and me. Her face went white as a sheet when she saw me standing there. For a minute, she was so shocked and embarrassed, she was obviously unable to speak, and then she blurted out her apologies.

"I am so sorry," she stammered. "Jane, I am so sorry." She ran to me and hugged me. "I didn't know you were here. Are you okay?"

"I invited Jane to stay with us," Mary said. "She can't stay at Thornfield anymore, and she obviously can't be anyplace with her name on the lease or anything. She can't risk that psycho finding her if he gets out on parole."

I hadn't thought about that. I hadn't thought that Edward could be dangerous. I couldn't imagine having to hide from him or being afraid of him. He was one of the only people I had ever felt safe with. He was the only person I had ever really been myself with.

"Of course, you'll stay with us," Sara said, as she gave me one more squeeze before pulling away. "You'll stay with us as long as you like."

"Thank you," I whispered.

"He didn't hurt you...did he?" Sara asked tentatively.

"No." My voice sounded strangled and I struggled not to cry again. "He was perfect. He was everything I ever...I can't imagine him hurting anyone. He was never anything but kind to me."

"I volunteered at the domestic violence shelter last summer," Mary said. "There's a cycle of violence, you know? It's always the guys who seem the most passionate who become the most violent. First, they romance you and sweep you off your feet, then they flip out when they think they might lose you or you "piss them off" by leaving a dirty dish on the table or something stupid like that. And then it starts again, and they're all lovey-dovey until they flip out again. The flipping out gets worse and worse over time. Thank God you never saw Edward flip out on you, Jane. Who knows what he would have done?"

I nodded. I didn't know how else to respond. What else could I do? I didn't believe Edward would ever hurt me, but all the evidence indicated he could have. I sat down on the sofa beside Sara's books.

"You know what we need to do?" Mary offered. "We need to go see a movie. Let's go see a movie."

Mary and Sara both grabbed me and took me out. They bought me popcorn and candy and we watched three movies. The local theater was playing a *Lord of the Rings* marathon, and we all sat quietly and lost ourselves in the fantasy. I was even able to forget about Edward for a while. It was just what I needed. I smiled and stuffed my face with popcorn. The world outside the theater melted away and all that existed was Middle Earth.

The movies ended, and reality came flooding back to me as I exited the theater. When we got back to the apartment, Sinjun was watching the news, and it wasn't good. Edward had made CNN. The anchor was talking about the Rochester family's long history of domestic abuse, wealth, and corruption. Murder, money, and cruelty had followed the family down through the centuries, culminating in this particularly heinous murder. Pictures of Bertha, and stories of her beauty and kindness, were part of the news story. I watched silently from the door. Mary and Sara were mesmerized by the coverage. The only thing I had to be grateful for was the fact that, somehow, my name was not part of the news. There was no information regarding the ordinary girl Edward Rochester had been dating. I took a deep breath in relief.

After far longer than necessary, Mary stepped forward and turned the television off.

"I was watching that," Sinjun protested.

"I don't think now is the time," Mary hissed.

Sinjun turned around and saw me. He stood up uncomfortably. He looked stiff. He shuffled his feet a bit. I'm sorry," he said. "I didn't realize you were here."

"It's okay," I said as I sat down. "I can't avoid the news forever."

Sinjun sat down next to me and gave me an awkward hug that was meant to be comforting. He smiled and put his arm around me. I leaned into him and felt the simple comfort from a nice guy.

"Are you okay?" he asked. "I knew that guy was bad news, but I had no idea. I tried to warn you, but I should have tried harder." Sinjun looked like he felt guilty. "I'm not good with things like that, but that guy must be a monster. I should have tried harder to help you."

"It isn't your fault," I whispered. I bit my lip trying not to cry. I couldn't stand it when people called Edward a monster. I could never believe he was a monster. It was like someone was pushing a knife into my gut. "I was the one who fell in love with him. I'm not naïve. I knew Edward had a difficult past."

I closed my eyes. I had known Edward wasn't all that he'd seemed. The signs had been everywhere. That night when Bertha's brother had gotten hurt., Edward had said the guy had fallen, but Edward must have stabbed him. The way Mrs. Fairfax had tried to warn me about him. Any idiot would have seen his extreme mood swings. It was odd that even then, none of that mattered to me. I still loved him. He was a part of my heart, now, and I couldn't escape him. Even knowing that he'd killed Bertha, I couldn't help but want to run to him. Maybe I was a monster, too? Or crazy like those desperate women who fall in love with prison inmates and end up on *Dr. Phil.*

Sinjun suggested we turn the TV back on and watch the news coverage so we could understand more about what had happened. I nodded and he flicked on the TV. He moved to the other chair and Sara and Mary sat on either side of me, burrowing close as though they would protect me from Edward, even through the TV set. The reporter was talking about The Rochester family. The men had always married young, and their brides usually ended up disappearing, dying, or going insane. Clearly, there was a long and sordid history of violence in the Rochester clan. Then they talked about Blanche Ingram, his most recent girlfriend, and how she'd been treated by Edward and was lucky to be alive. The girls grabbed my hands thinking they were going to mention me, and then a picture of Blanche flashed on the screen and they cut to an interview with her looking as beautiful as ever. She was crying. Her eyes were heavy with tears.

"We were going to be married this summer," she sobbed. "I am so grateful that they caught him when they did or I could have been next. I loved him so much." She buried her face in her hands and cried, but the tears seemed fake to me.

"What a bitch!" I spat involuntarily.

Everyone turned to face me in surprise, but I couldn't help myself. I continued on. "He dumped her before Christmas. He didn't even like her. He was mine!"

I stood up, trembling with rage. It was Mary who put her arms around me and sat me back down. "It's okay," she said softly. "It is normal for abused women to continue loving their abusers. It will take time for you to forget him. In the shelter, where I volunteered, women would go back to their abusers two or three times before they finally realized what monsters they were with. You are lucky he's in jail and you can't go back to him. Just remind yourself of how much he hurt you and how dangerous he is."

I took Mary's hand and said thank you, but I couldn't remember Edward ever being cruel or dangerous. I remembered him walking into the fire to save me. I remembered him carrying his grandmother, lovingly, to bed. I remembered him brushing his horse and whispering sweetly to it. These things were emblazoned in my mind like a seal upon my heart. I closed my eyes and realized those memories would have to stay locked in my heart because no one else would ever understand.

# CHAPTER 20

*And the sun that warmed our stooping
backs and withered the weed uprooted.
We shall not see it again. We shall all die in
darkness and be buried in the rain.*

~ Edna St. Vincent Millay

I TRIED TO AVOID THE news from then on. I focused
on school and preparations for our summer trip. I focused
on my finals. I got another part-time job working in the
university library. Mary and Sinjun and Sara became my
family. We did everything together. They even threw a party
for me when I turned seventeen. I was more grateful for
them than I had ever been for anyone. I would have gone
crazy without them.

The semester ended and Sinjun graduated. I sat and
watched him walk across the stage. He didn't like big
parties, so we had a small dinner for him. His parents
came. They were lovely people, who spent far too much
time talking to me. They asked me about my past and
my future goals. Sinjun put his hand on mine during

the dinner and smiled at me. I smiled back. He was a good friend.

That week, strange news greeted me. The library had kept me on for the summer, and I had just finished a shift and was relaxing on the couch watching a movie. It was nice sometimes just to veg out. I was learning from Sara and Mary that I didn't need to spend every waking hour studying. That I could relax, once in a while. And besides, the year was over and I had gotten straight As. It was summer and since we only had A/C window units in the bedrooms, the rest of the apartment was hot, so I was wearing shorts and a tank top and had two fans going.

The doorbell rang and I answered it, expecting it to be one of Mary or Sara's boyfriends, but instead, it was a short, bald man in a neatly pressed suit, and a tall woman with white hair in a severe blunt cut, large glasses, and a bright orange dress.

"Are you Miss Jane Marsh? Formerly of Gateshead, Massachusetts?"

"Y-yes, what can I do for you?" I asked, my mind already spinning into worry mode.

"My name is Richard Crumbly and I am an attorney representing your uncle, Cerrus Blackbriar, and this is Ms. Tara Brocklehurst, from Child Protective Services."

"Oh," I said. I was slightly stunned.

I invited them in and made some tea. Ms. Brocklehurst looked around at our messy apartment with a shriveled nose. Mary had had a party the night before and beer bottles lined the tiny coffee table. Old pizza boxes were on the floor, too.

"We have some very important matters to discuss with you, Jane," Mr. Crumbly stated, taking a seat on the couch.

"Well," Ms. Brocklehurst announced, "your foster mother passed away and your custody was returned to the state."

I knew Mrs. Blankenship had been close to the end the last time I saw her, but it was a shock to hear the words that she had died. "I'm sorry to hear that." That was all I could muster. "What does it mean that my custody has been returned to the state?"

"Look around you. You are a seventeen-year-old girl living with college students who have parties on a regular basis, judging from all these beer bottles. I discovered from speaking to Mrs. Blankenship's former hospice care nurse, that you had been living and working at the Thornfield estate since last summer when you were only sixteen. Further investigation at Thornfield revealed that, since Christmas, you had been dating the Rochester family heir, Edward Rochester, and sleeping with him in his quarters, without any proper chaperone or supervision. And that you were set to fly off to Florida with him before he was arrested for murdering a previous girlfriend. Your arms are covered in tattoos and God only knows how many you have elsewhere on your body. What do you think the state should do with a girl like you?"

I looked down. The tattoo had spread to my lower arms. I hadn't even noticed. I grabbed a cardigan that was hanging on the hook by the door and put it on. "It isn't like that," I answered.

"Isn't it? If it weren't for your attorney, I would be sending you to a home for troubled teens. You should know that is what I recommended. You are out of control."

"My attorney?" I asked stupidly.

"I am your attorney," Crumbly said. "Your uncle put me in charge of finding you and making sure you were safe and taken care of. After Mrs. Blankenship's death, we decided to intervene."

I swallowed the lump in my throat. I had only found out about my uncle when I went to see Mrs. Blankenship but, with everything that had happened, I hadn't even bothered trying to contact him.

"You did receive the money he sent, didn't you? Why didn't you contact him?" the attorney asked in a stern voice. "He sent a detailed letter with his contact information to Mrs. Blankenship."

"I never got the money. My foster mother told me about it. She spent it. But she didn't tell me my uncle wanted to meet me."

The attorney shook his head. "Mr. Blackbriar was so sorry about how you were treated in foster care. You see, Mr. Blackbriar's younger sister, your mother, was a run-away. She had been missing from the age of fourteen and it took a long time for your uncle to find you. It was his greatest regret, knowing he had let his sister's daughter get lost in a system of abuse and neglect."

Ms. Brocklehurst bristled at this. "Mr. Crumbly, there are thousands of good people who are foster parents and give nothing but love and support to the children they take in."

Mr. Crumbly glanced at Ms. Brocklehurst with a condescending smile. "There are also many people who take advantage of the money they get from the government and abuse the children they are supposed to be loving and supporting." Mr. Crumbly turned back to me, his expression softening. "Your uncle wanted me to tell you how sorry he was that you had to go through so much in your young life."

"Okay," I said. "Well, that's good to hear, at least." I was having trouble processing everything.

"There is more. Your uncle wants to make amends for what you have gone through."

"Amends? What happened to me wasn't his fault. . ." I began.

"It is already done, my dear. It is already done. He is in the process of adopting you and making you his heir. Everything he has will be yours when he dies."

"What?"

"He is quite well off. He doesn't have any children of his own. He has set up a bank account in your name, with regular deposits to cover your various expenses. You *will* have to leave Huntington. He wouldn't have forced this condition, but Ms. Brocklehurst here, representing the organization that completely lost track of you, is demanding you be in the care of an adult. They don't want you to be unsupervised."

"What?" I asked again stupidly.

The attorney handed me a thick manila envelope. "All the details are in here."

"We did not lose track of her!" Ms. Brocklehurst protested. Her pale face turned bright red with anger. "She was in the care of a foster mother. We had documentation showing she was being properly cared for. How were we supposed to know that your client was a liar and a delinquent?"

Mr. Crumbly turned on Ms. Brocklehurst. He was fierce when he got angry. "You didn't lose her? You had no idea where she was. When Mrs. Blankenship, died, you didn't even know she was no longer residing there. You wanted to treat her like a run-away instead of an honor student with a full scholarship to a prestigious university. She is no delinquent and her uncle wants to make it clear that you are not to refer to her in this way. I would also note, Ms. Brocklehurst, that we are considering launching a lawsuit against the state, along with possible criminal charges. We have evidence showing that Jane was placed in a foster home, at the tender age of five, with a pedophile that caused the death one of the other children in his care. If that isn't a neglectful system, I don't know what is."

"That was an unfortunate circumstance and we had no way of knowing he was a pedophile. He was screened and passed several psychological evaluations prior to becoming a foster parent."

"Stop!" I yelled. "Are you kidding me? You two are taking me out of school? I am going on a trip to Haiti in two weeks. What about that??" I was standing up now and shaking. I had come too far, and I had worked too hard, to quit. "This has to be a joke!"

"I assure you, this is no joke," Ms. Brocklehurst exclaimed. "You need proper adult supervision. You are a minor. You are changing schools and there is no way you are leaving the country."

"I can't leave school!" I yelled. "I'm studying pre-med, I can't—"

Ms. Brocklehurst interrupted. "You will not be leaving school, but things are definitely going to change for you, young lady!"

"The state expressed concern at your recent living arrangements and your lack of guidance with a guardian," Crumbly interjected. "You have to live with your uncle. And don't worry about your education, you will be attending a fine university in New York. You won't lose any of your credits."

"How can all of this have happened without me even knowing? I should have been notified!" I glared at both of them. "How could you do this without my permission! You don't even know me!"

Ms. Brocklehurst cleared her throat. "I wanted to come for you two weeks ago, but Mr. Crumbly, here, took us to court and argued that you needed to finish school."

"Well, thanks for that, at least," I grumbled.

Crumbly nodded. "You are lucky, Jane. CPS wanted to have you reassigned to inpatient care. They were reviewing your case, for immediate relocation. You were a minor, living with an adult male, who has been charged with murder. They could have put you in a group home. It was only because of our intervention that this didn't happen."

My mouth hung open. I couldn't find anything to say.

"We will give you one week to get your affairs in order and pack your things. After that week is up, we will escort you to New York City, where you will take up residence with your Uncle Cerrus. I will also monitor you regularly and provide you with a monthly allowance until you come of age. Your allowance will be $5,000 a month. I trust that will be sufficient?"

My mouth dropped open.

Mr. Crumbly evidently took that as a "yes" and continued. "Your uncle has also provided you with a $25,000 check to cover any relocation expenses such as the shipping of your belongings."

I didn't think I could spend that much money in a year let alone spend it on shipping what few possessions I owned. "Will I get to meet my Uncle Cerrus?" I finally asked. "It seems kind of ironic that I'm in trouble for living with an adult male and I'm being forced to move in with another adult male, whom I've never met. How do you know he's even my uncle?"

Mr. Crumbly smiled. "I promise you that this woman," he signaled to Ms. Brocklehurst, "and her department have put Mr. Blackbriar through every hoop imaginable. He has been approved for adoption. Mr. Blackbriar is a wealthy man, who made his fortune managing a hedge fund, retired young, and now travels the world finding unique artifacts for wealthy collectors. And you may appreciate that he is a collector, himself, of rare books and antiquities. I can assure you, Jane, you will be happier than you've ever been, living with your uncle."

"I haven't even met him," I said softly.

"He will meet with you after you arrive in New York."

"I need more than a week to get my school stuff together. It isn't easy to transfer."

"We have arranged for you to transfer to Barnard College, in New York. Everything has been taken care of."

Mr. Crumbly was efficient, I'd give him that.

He handed me another thick envelope. I opened it and leafed through it. All the legal documents were in the envelope. There was a check written out to me. There was the address of my new home and all the contact information for everyone involved in my case, including Ms. Brocklehurst. It was all so official and final. I had no choice in any of this. It was overwhelming, to say the least, but then, my life had been one big roller coaster ride the past year.

Mr. Crumbly and Ms. Brocklehurst left without saying much more and I went to the bank to deposit the check. I stood there staring at the teller and it was when I got the deposit slip in my hand that it really hit me. I had money. I had real money and I had people looking out for me. There were people I could call for help if I was hungry or cold or homeless. I would never have to worry, again. I stared into the teller's eyes and laughed. I laughed like a crazy person. The teller must have thought I was as mad as a hatter, but she only smiled.

It was all starting to sink in. I vowed to myself I wouldn't live any differently. I wouldn't tell anyone about my change in finances. I would keep my budget slim and save the money for school and for my future. But it was like a weight had been lifted from my chest. I wouldn't have to scramble for part-time jobs. I could devote myself completely to my studies and not have to live on mac and cheese and cans of tomato soup like I did when I was in high school.

I decided not to tell anyone about my leaving. I pretended it wasn't happening and just let life go on like it always had. I figured Sinjun was leaving for Vanderbilt, and the girls were already looking for a more affordable apartment, so they would be more relieved than stressed by my news. I would be sad when I had to say goodbye. I had grown really close to them all, and they had supported me through everything.

# CHAPTER 21

*Something wicked this way comes.*

~ William Shakespeare

THE DAY BEFORE I LEFT, I asked Sinjun to go out with me to the old cemetery behind the Biology building. The sun shone over the tombstones making them glow with an otherworldly light. It reminded me of Thornfield. The cemetery felt full old ghosts and lost souls. I missed my ghosts. I missed all my ghosts. I still hadn't told Sinjun and Mary and Sara about my having to leave. I was having trouble finding the words to tell them I couldn't go to Haiti and I couldn't stay with them.

"I'll be leaving for Vanderbilt after we get back from Haiti," Sinjun said into the awkward silence.

"I know," I said with a sad smile. "I'm going to miss you."

At this, Sinjun grabbed me and pulled me to him. I was too stunned to react. I just looked up into his eyes like a deer caught in the headlights. "I am so glad to hear you say that," he said. "I have had feelings for you for so long, I didn't want to say anything. I wanted to give you time to recover, but I can't think of going anywhere without you. When you asked me out on this date, it was the best day of my life."

I opened my mouth, but no words came out. I had no idea Sinjun had felt this way about me. I was stunned.

"I've thought a lot about it and you could transfer with me next semester. We could get a place together and I would take care of you. You wouldn't have to worry about money. It would be okay. Edward could never find you. I love you."

Sinjun leaned down to kiss me and I pushed him away. I couldn't kiss him. I was Edward's. The look on Sinjun's face was crushing. He looked like I had punched him.

"I'm sorry Sinjun," I whispered. "I just can't."

"Why? Why can't you?" he demanded. "Why did you even ask me out if you weren't interested in me?"

"I didn't think this was a date! I just needed to tell you something important. I am sorry if I misled you, but I can't date anyone."

"Because of him?" he demanded. "Because of that criminal, who murdered his girlfriend and set her on fire? You can't still love him? Not after everything he did? Jane, you are broken!"

The wind whispered through the gravestones and the clouds shifted and eclipsed the sun. The skull on the tombstone next to me stared up at me with its empty eyes.

"I'm not broken. And that's a terrible thing to say."

"I love you." He grabbed me by my shoulders. "We've been friends for almost a year and I've loved you that entire time. I know that jerk broke your heart. I can see it in your eyes, but I know that if you come with me you'll learn to love me." His eyes were staring into mine with such intensity, it scared me. "We have so much in common, Jane. We have the same calling in life. We can travel the world together and work with Doctors Without Borders and really make a difference in the world. You are the only girl I have ever met with the same drive and passion I have."

I shrugged off his hands and stepped back. "There is more to me than hard work and a desire to make a difference."

"No, I see that in your eyes. I see what you are. You are good and strong and that man led you astray. But I know the right man can put you back on the right path. You're a good person. You have your entire life ahead of you."

I backed away even farther. The wind howled. It shrieked. "I am not who you think I am. I loved Edward because his soul and mine were alike. I have ghosts in my past. Darkness that you can never begin to understand. I have a calling, yes, but I also want passion and love in my life. I have seen too many people settle and I just won't accept that fate for myself."

Sinjun looked at me as if he were seeing me for the first time. The wind swirled and howled around us. A look of pain crossed his face, then his lips compressed into a thin, tight line. "I thought you were different." His eyes were cold. "But you're just a silly little girl."

The wind cried out again and I turned away from him. I could hear a howling from far away. I could hear it calling my name. It grew louder, echoing all around me. It was Edward.

"Jane," the voice called. "Jane! Come back to me."

A gust of wind whipped my hair around my face, I turned into it. Letting it surround me, embrace me. "I'm coming!" I answered.

"Edward! I'm coming."

Sinjun grabbed me and pulled me away from the wind and out of my trance. "Have you lost your mind?" he demanded.

I smiled. "I did lose my mind." I shook my head. "I'm sorry Sinjun, but I should never have left Edward. It was crazy to leave him when he needed me most. I'm going to find him before I lose my chance at true happiness."

# CHAPTER 22

*I shall never sleep calmly again when I think of the horrors that lurk ceaselessly behind life in time and in space.*

~ H.P. Lovecraft

IT WAS WELL PAST DARK when I got back to the apartment. The moon was high in the sky and the night air was cool, despite the fact that it was May. I was exhausted, but I couldn't rest. I went to my little room in the apartment and spent some time getting dressed and doing my hair and makeup. I wanted to look nice. I wanted to look the way Edward always made me feel. I wanted to be beautiful. I became aware that I wasn't even sure if Edward was still living at Thornfield. I had avoided the news for so long that I had no idea what had happened to him. He could be in prison. He could be in New York. He could have fled to France and be hiding in some country estate of his family's to avoid extradition, for all I knew.

The tears began to flow. They bubbled up and poured down my cheeks in an unstoppable current. There would be no sleep for me. I walked out into the cool night air with a purpose. I got into my trusty old Jeep and started driving. I may not know where Edward was, but I knew where Thornfield was. Mrs. Fairfax had to know how to find him. I set out toward the estate with a fixed purpose. I wiped my tears away and kept driving until I saw the towering spires of the only place I had ever felt at home.

As I caught my first glimpse of the old manor, my heart dropped like a rock. My breath left my chest and I felt like I might suffocate under the weight of my own overwhelming emotions. I drove up to the gate and got out. I opened it and continued on, hoping that what stood before me was a mirage, built by my sleep-deprived mind. The closer I got to Thornfield, the more I knew what I was seeing was real.

The house was still standing, in places. The façade still faced out, with its bleak and gothic beauty, but the roof was gone and the stone walls were charred. The windows were shattered and the doors had been burnt away. I parked a few yards away, got out, and walked slowly toward the entrance. The smell of smoke and cinder still lingered in the air. The front door had been ripped from the hinges, so I didn't need a key. I stepped inside and walked into the foyer. The walls were charred and blackened. Most of the furniture and old paintings were smothered by what was left of the roof. The once beautiful staircase led up to nothing.

I placed my hand over my mouth and sank to my knees. I think I would have sat there forever if it weren't for the light that made me turn. I saw her in the darkness. She was there, as she had always been there. Liliana. She placed a

140

spectral hand on my shoulder. I couldn't feel it. I wasn't even sure if what I was seeing was real. I wondered if I hadn't slipped into madness.

"He is alive," Liliana said softly.

"What?" I asked quietly.

"My lord wouldn't let him die. He still needs him... and you." She seemed so sad.

"What happened here?" I had started to sob. I was insane. I knew I had to be. I was lying in the dirt talking to a ghost.

"The house caught on fire. It was Bertha."

"So, Edward did murder her?"

Liliana smiled. "No, my dear, he did not. She stabbed him and he fought back. She wouldn't stop and they struggled. He stabbed at her three times before she finally quieted. Then, when he sat back, crying in agony, she kicked him down the stairs. She set herself on fire and leapt through the window. She wanted him dead."

"Why did she do that?"

Lilliana laughed. "The curse drove her insane."

"Where is he now?" I asked.

"He's in New York. He was kicked out of Yale. But they dropped the charges. Mrs. Fairfax had witnessed everything and testified on his behalf in court."

"Are you real? How do you know all this if you are a ghost?"

"Am I a ghost?" she asked as if she was confused. "I think I am still in hell and you are here to torture me. You are here to remind me of my sins, beautiful Jane. I know this because my lord wants me to know this. He wants me to see all that I have set into motion. He wants me to see you. He is coming for you."

My lips went numb and my heartbeat slowed. The blood drained from my face. "What?" I asked stupidly.

"Time is a strange thing. In the Shadowlands, it flows back and forth. I forget when and where I am, but I know you, daughter. Your father has a job for you."

"You are crazy, or maybe I am crazy. I am talking to a dead woman. I am probably crazy."

"Maybe," she said with a gentle smile. "Maybe everything I said is a lie. Maybe we are both insane or, maybe, the thing that was written on you when they found you in that hospital is true. Maybe love is the key. Go find your Edward. See if you can still love him now that he has been altered." Her smile wasn't sweet anymore. It was cruel.

"Altered?"

"He was in the house when it burned down. He had brought his grandmother back home to live with him. He tried to save her and was pinned in the fire. Miss Adele died and he was injured. The flesh is so easily peeled away. Beauty, so easily destroyed."

My heart was breaking. Miss Adele had died in the fire. And Edward was injured and scarred. He was good. He wasn't evil. He was good and brave, and I hated myself for not believing him.

I stood up and wiped the tears from my eyes. "I don't care."

Liliana scowled. "We will see. I once loved a man like that, but it was not meant to be." There were flames in her dark eyes. "Love is like a fire that destroys all it touches. It will consume you, too."

"It wouldn't matter," I answered. "Let it burn me. I don't care."

Liliana faded. She was only a whisper of light. "You think this is the end. You think the Devil died in this fire, but this is only the beginning. He will come for you. He always comes for what is his."

The phantom faded and the light went with her. I looked up and saw the red lady, Bertha, staring down at me from the stairs. The house was hers now. It belonged to her, alone. She laughed at me from her shadowy perch and then vanished. I was left standing alone, in the dark, covered in soot, and praying that everything Liliana had said was madness.

# CHAPTER 23

*It was not the thorn bending to the
honeysuckles, but the honeysuckles
embracing the thorn.*

~ Emily Bronte

THE NEXT NIGHT I KNEW I had to tell Sara and
Mary about everything. Sinjun was hiding in his room.
Mary and Sara were packing for the Haiti trip. They still
thought I was going.

They sat on the sofa and I brought them each a drink.
"I have to leave tomorrow," I told them.

"What?" Sara asked in disbelief.

"CPS came for me. I am an unsupervised minor."

"That is insane. We're watching out for you," Mary
said. "We can vouch for you, and you're the most responsible person we know."

"It isn't that easy. When they came to find me, there
were beer bottles everywhere and they are holding the
whole Rochester thing against me. I have to do what they
say. It could have been worse."

"Where are they taking you?" Sara asked as she took my hand.

"I'm going to live with an uncle in New York."

Both girls sat in stunned silence. Finally, Mary spoke, "Maybe it's for the best, Jane. I don't want to sound terrible, but you are just barely seventeen and some family support wouldn't hurt you. You could have ended up homeless after the Rochester thing. We want to take care of you, but I'm only twenty. I can't. We couldn't even afford an apartment with a room for you." Mary put her hand on mine. "We were really stressing out about it. We aren't equipped to take care of you. Family will be good for you."

"And we will come visit you every break!" Sara said. "I love New York. You won't be alone. I will text you and email you."

I hadn't realized how much of a burden I had been on the girls, until that moment. They had felt responsible for me. They felt like they had to care for me. I hugged them both. It was for the best...and Edward was there. I could find Edward in New York if I could just slip under CPS's radar.

"Thank you, both." I was choking up again. "You have no idea how much your friendship has meant to me. I believe this is for the best. I just hope we won't drift apart."

Sara threw her arms around me. "There is no way we will drift apart!"

We spent the night packing and eating sushi. I was going to miss my friends. Sinjun stayed carefully tucked away in his room. I never saw him again.

That night I didn't get any sleep. How could I? I was standing on the precipice of a new life. I had stood on this precipice many times before. I knew it well. After three foster homes, living at Thornfield, and then moving in with the girls, the only constant in my life had been the knowledge that everything I knew and trusted could be yanked out from under my feet in a heartbeat. Every time I had begun to feel safe and secure in any environment, that sense of security was snatched out from under me. So, I sat awake all night, wondering what new wonders or terrors awaited me in my new home, and figuring out how I was going to get away and find Edward.

Ms. Brocklehurst and Mr. Crumbly showed up at 7:00 a.m. to escort me to the airport. The girls woke up and hugged me. They cried but somehow tears eluded me. It was as if I didn't have any tears left. Ms. Brocklehurst and Mr. Crumbly were quiet and stiff for our entire journey. They made me feel like I was being escorted to jail. The two sat in uncomfortable silence, on either side of me, for the entire plane ride. Ms. Brocklehurst walked with me to the bathroom when I had to go. It was like she expected me to try to sprint for the emergency exit.

When we landed, she didn't let me out of her sight for a second. She practically sat on my lap for the entire cab ride. I tried to pretend I wasn't on my way to potential lockdown. I had no idea what my uncle was like or what his expectations would be. It was entirely possible that I would have to sneak out my window to try to find Edward. I had never really felt like a normal teenager. I had never felt constricted by rules or trapped in my age. I had never had any rules and if I had, there would never have been any reason to break them. I suddenly felt like how all those girls I hated in high school must have felt. I had looked at them with disdain when I heard them talking about breaking rules or sneaking out for a boy. I finally understood them. I understood what it felt like to be a prisoner of your age.

# CHAPTER 24

*I cannot live without my life! I cannot live
without my soul!*

~ Emiy Bronte

DESPITE MY BROODING, I COULDN'T help but
become increasingly aware of the city we were driving
through. We drove over the Brooklyn Bridge and New
York surrounded us like a living organism. There was life
everywhere. People crowded the sidewalks and traffic came
to a standstill. Buildings towered above us like testaments
to the innovation of civilization. My worries began to fade
as I became mesmerized by the landscape. We turned by
Central Park and I got a view of lush green trees and fairy
tale playgrounds. We turned down a street lined with beautiful brownstone buildings, and I watched in wonder as
the busy city landscape transformed into a quiet, elegant
neighborhood.

When we finally arrived at my uncle's townhouse, I
practically sprinted to the door I was so desperate to escape
my new wardens. The townhouse was a magnificent old

home of dark red brick with a stately front door, painted in a glossy dark red. A beautiful fountain featured three young women holding hands in a circle. They wore long flowing robes and wreaths of flowers in their hair. The fountain was situated on the small patch of green that made up the front yard.

Mr. Crumbly let us in and my two wardens allowed me to explore while they bickered about details and made phone calls.

The inside was not so magnificent and definitely strange. It didn't feel like a house at all. It felt like something out of a circus sideshow or a morbid gothic museum. It was filled with artifacts that looked as if they had come from other worlds. Skeletons and bones littered bookshelves, and statues of strange gods and pagan monsters cluttered the tops of tables. I wandered in and out of rooms, filled with shelves of old skulls and shrunken heads and ancient vases, and tried to pull myself together. The oddity of the place helped me with this. The townhouse's vast open spaces and cold stone floors echoed with the sound of old and dead objects. Tiny skeletons of malformed children stood in glass cases next to ancient relics that claimed magical powers. The townhouse was massive for the Upper West side of New York. It was at least 7,000 square feet of rooms, filled with strange junk covered in dust. There were three bedrooms, a kitchen, and three bathrooms, but the rest of the place was ominously useless. I focused on the old objects and tried to steady my breath. I closed my eyes and tried to remind myself to be calm.

I found what was clearly meant to be my room and began unpacking. Time lingered. Ms. Brocklehurst and Mr. Crumbly were yelling in an old room filled with pagan dolls. Their voices echoed through the silence. I could tell Ms. Brocklehurst was upset that my uncle hadn't met us at the door, but I couldn't fix that. The room that was meant to be mine was clearly set up for a much younger girl. It was pink and had flowers on the wallpaper. The bedspread had tiny roses and there were teddy bears and stuffed animals on the bed. It was the bedroom I would have begged for when I was seven. I lay down on the pink bed and found myself oddly at peace. I drifted off and when I awoke, I could hear them still fighting. I stayed tucked away in my room and waited. Finally, Mr. Crumbly knocked on the door. He escorted me down to the massive kitchen.

When I first saw my uncle, my impulse was to run. He smiled brightly, but every part of me wanted to head for the door. Of course, that wasn't an option, so I stood quietly and studied my new legal guardian. I knew his face well. I had seen it in a hundred dreams and nightmares. He had dark skin and dark hair. He looked young, too young to be my uncle. His face was angular, with very high cheekbones and his eyes were dark. If he'd had yellow eyes, skin made of wood, and horns, he would have been Liliana's Dark Lord.

"I am your Uncle Cerrus," he said, extending his hand.

"I'm Jane," I responded without taking his hand.

"Sorry I was late. I had things to do. Thank the gods for Crumbly, otherwise that stupid cu…bitch would have taken you away." He smiled again. A perfect smile, with perfect teeth. Why did it creep me out? "You can leave, Crumbly. I'll call you if I need you."

Crumbly bowed. He bowed to my uncle like a serf and ran out of the townhouse like my uncle was King Henry VIII. We stood in awkward silence. I felt small and helpless and he looked completely pleased with himself. He was smiling from ear to ear.

"You aren't my uncle."

# CHAPTER 25

*Who Knows the end?*

~ H.P. Lovecraft

"I AM CERRUS."

"What are you? Twenty-five years old at the most? You are not my uncle."

"Why would you say that?" He seemed more curious than offended.

"I know you."

"Really? How specifically?"

I ran. I sprinted toward the exit, but there was no way out. He was waiting for me at the front door. He stood calmly, blocking the door with the same stupid smile plastered on his face. But with one difference. His eyes were no longer brown. They were yellow.

"Don't you want to know who you are, Jane?" he asked. "Don't you want to know who you really are?"

"Let me out."

"Jane. Lovely Jane." He was still smiling. "You can't leave. I adopted you. You are legally mine."

I shuddered. My skin was cold. The only warmth on my body radiated from the tattoos that now covered my entire back. I couldn't fight him. He was right. I had to stay with him.

"I know that," I said quietly.

"Would you like to know who you really are?" His voice was a caress. It hissed its way through the room like a serpent. I could feel it slithering up my spine.

"What are you talking about?"

"Or have you figured it out already and you don't want to believe it?"

"I am Jane Marsh."

"No." His eyes flashed with a yellow fire. "You are not Jane Marsh. That is their name. You are not one of them and you have never been. You are *my* Jane. Jane of the morning. Daughter of the Air Spirits. Ghosts follow you and curses are lifted in your presence. You are a daughter of the old ones. You are mine."

"You're crazy. Check yourself into rehab and let me out!" I backed away from him and saw the masks on the walls smiling, too. Their hollow eyes flashed yellow fire. I couldn't breathe. My heart was pounding in my head. The room started spinning around me. He reached out and grabbed me by the shoulders and I saw his horns. The horns on his head. I screamed and then everything went black.

I woke up in my pink bed in my pink room. Something cool was on my forehead. And someone was sitting beside me, holding my hand.

"Are you okay, Jane?"

It was Cerrus. He was gazing at me in concern. The horns were gone and his eyes were brown, again.

"You-you said I was a daughter of the air, of the old ones. What does that mean? What do you want with me?

"You must be tired; you've been through so much Jane…You're overwrought…"

He squeezed my hand. "Do you want me to call a doctor?"

I shook my head. "Who are you, really?"

"I'm your uncle and your legal guardian. You're safe Jane. There is nothing to be afraid of."

My breathing began to steady. I must have had one major freak-out session. Cerrus looked just like the horned man from my dreams. I must have imagined he'd said those things. I was tired. I was stressed. I wasn't making sense. I had panicked; that must have been it.

"I'm sorry," I said in a shaky whisper.

Cerrus helped me sit up. "No, don't be sorry. I'm sorry for scaring you."

"You are truly my uncle?"

"I am family. I was there when you were born."

"Then why did you leave me?" I hadn't realized how angry I was. "Why did you abandon me when I was a little kid? They said my mother ran away from home and was in a cult…" I was acting like a crazy person again, but I was having trouble controlling my own emotions.

"I never left you. I have always watched over you. And those are just stories, told by people like Ms. Brocklehurst,

155

who need to cover up their mistakes. It was horrible what happened to you. But you're safe now.

I tried to calm myself. "So, what now?" I asked. I was still crying, but at least I wasn't hysterical.

"Now, you don't need to worry about anything. Go to school. Find happiness. I will take care of you.

You just need to check in with me daily. Crumbly will stop by once a month and Brocklehurst will be with him, so I'll be here for those visits. But I won't stifle you or try to cage you in. You are an amazing young woman. You've done fine on your own, so far. I see no reason to scare you or force you to change the way you live. I won't bother you. I'm hardly ever here, anyway."

I covered my face with my hands. "I'm not comfortable with this."

"You have been through so much worse, Jane. This is a small hurdle. You were brought here for a reason."

"What does that mean?"

"You have to find Edward. True love awaits."

"How do you know about him! They told me to stay away from him."

"I am not *they*, Jane. I am Cerrus. I will protect you from them."

Nothing he said made any sense. He was so weird and utterly off-putting.

"This world is only a dream, sweet Jane, and everything up until now has been a nightmare. Nothing will be as it was. I promise you, that you will never be afraid again…Come, I want to give you something." He helped me up and led me back downstairs to a sitting room, just off the foyer.

He went to a shelf lined with old books and various artifacts and picked up a small wooden box. He placed it in the palm of my hand. "Open it."

Inside, was a handwritten note. It looked like something that had been lost in time, but I recognized the handwriting and the paper it was written on. It was Liliana's. "Love is the gateway. Love is the key that will set the old ones free."

"What does it mean?" I whispered.

"I wrote those words on you when I left you at the hospital."

Fear vanished and something else crept in. Rage. "Why would you do that?" I yelled. "What does it mean?"

"You were right," he said. "I am not your uncle…I am your father."

All thought fled from me. I felt like a seven-year-old girl again, back in Mrs. Reed's home when I had to stand up to John Reed, the bully. I was ready to do battle. All the years I had spent hiding my emotions and keeping myself calm and rational vanished. I was young and wild, and I couldn't contemplate anything beside the moment I was in. I punched Cerrus hard in the face. "Why?" I demanded with clenched fists.

He grinned at my paltry attempt at violence. "Because my beautiful daughter, you are the *one*. You are the door to the past and the future."

"Are you mentally ill? What does that even mean?"

"You have to accept that magic is real. Ghosts are real and, just outside this flimsy thing you call reality, there are universes teeming with gods and monsters and magic and beauty and horror. You have to let go of everything and know, in your heart, that there is power in you that is so old and so magnificent that kings and presidents will fall to their knees and shake at the sight of it."

"You're full of bullshit!" My face was flushed with anger. "How do you expect me to believe what you're telling me, let alone accept it."

"You can accept it because you know that it is true. You know that I am the horned king from your dreams and that I am your father. You know that everything you have ever done, or will do, was fashioned by the gods. The tattoo on your back is calling to you. Edward is calling to you." He stepped out of the room and pointed to the front door. "Go. Answer the call. Open the door. Let your passion set you free to be who you were born to be."

I shook my head.

Cerrus laughed. "Sweet daughter, I am not here to upset you. Take your time. I have traveled through time and space to bring you here. Time doesn't matter. Find joy. Spend money. Go shopping. There is an amazing library here. Read. Go see a play."

He handed me a check card. "Everything you ever wanted is yours now. There is nothing you can't do or have." He handed me a piece of paper with an address on it.

"What is this?"

"Edward."

I took the paper. The address was only three houses down.

You can't escape who you are and what your destiny is Jane. Edward is part of it.

Had Cerrus spoken or had I said those words to myself?

I looked up. Cerrus had vanished, which made me even more furious and confused.

# CHAPTER 26

*The Old Ones were, the Old Ones are, and the Old Ones shall be. Not in the spaces we know, but between them. They walk serene and prima, undimensioned, and to us unseen.*

~ H.P.Lovecraft

I SAT ON THE FLOOR of the foyer with my back against the front door and pulled my knees up to my chest. I remembered the dream I had about the old house with the red front door. The door to Cerrus's townhouse was red. Everything I had feared was happening. I wanted to curse and scream. I wanted to yell, but instead, I sat curled up in a ball and quietly tried to make sense of everything. I looked down at my arms. The vines from my tattoo had moved down to my wrists. I looked at the paper with Edward's address on it. Without thinking, I stood up and opened the door. I stepped outside into the sunshine and walked to Edward's house and found myself staring up at the elegant brownstone.

All I wanted was to ring the doorbell and make Edward mine again. All I wanted was to do all the things

I had spent my entire life trying not to do. I wanted to take him up to the bedroom and do the things that got teenage girls into trouble, but I couldn't get the image of Cerrus out of my head. He wanted me to have sex with Edward. He wanted me to do this. Why? I looked up at the brownstone, again, and I saw something sitting by the door. I wasn't afraid. I should have been, but I wasn't. The creature that sat on the door was twisted and warped. It was covered in eyes and tongues and matted black fur. I could smell it. It occurred to me that I was losing my mind. I was hallucinating. I was insane. I couldn't go to Edward. I couldn't even see straight.

I went home and crawled into my pink bed. Sleep came too quickly and dreams came with sleep. I saw myself standing in the tower, in Thornfield. Edward was in front of me and I had a knife in my hand. I was stabbing him repeatedly. I laughed diabolically and then Edward burst into flames. The tattoo had spread out and covered my entire body. It wrapped me in ivy and skulls and death, and the fire flowed out of me like a river. Edward screamed and I just laughed.

I woke up to fire. I was on fire, but I wasn't burning. I stood up quickly and began putting the fire out with my blanket. The fire stopped and everything looked singed.

"What if it was always you?" a voice said from the corner. I jumped and backed away.

"Who's there?" I demanded.

Helen stepped out into the light. She looked different. She looked subdued. Her hair was long again. She wasn't wearing any makeup and all she had on was a white summer dress. "It is just me," Helen said softly. "What if it was always you?"

"What?" I asked.

She looked different. She looked faded and broken. She looked like a ghost.

"I'm so sorry, Jane," Helen whispered.

I ran to her as she began to cry. I tried to wrap my arms around her like before, but I couldn't. She was different. She was smoke. She was fog. She was a phantom.

"Why are you sorry?" I asked.

"I tried so hard to get you to leave, but I would have set you on fire if I knew what I know now. That would have been better than what I have led you to."

"Why?" I begged.

"I have to show you the truth," she said in between sobs. "I wish I didn't have to, but I have to try to save you, to save everyone, one last time."

She grabbed me and her phantom hand burned into my flesh. I closed my eyes. I was terrified, but the truth was there as it always had been. I remembered everything. Cerrus was my father. I remembered him holding me as a child. His arms were like wood, dark and strong. He raised me in the Shadowlands. He raised me in that dark place where the old ones lived. I couldn't see all of it. I could only remember bits. I remember an old tree that I would climb into. It was massive and dark and covered in knots, and inside it was lit up like a Christmas tree. I would sit in the tree and talk to Aylith, a woman with yellow eyes and lips. She would tell stories of the time before time when the great old ones walked with men. I didn't understand much. I smiled because Aylith was beautiful. She was the one who kissed my back and planted the seed that grew into the door on my back. I had never questioned anything when Cerrus took me from my home and left me in a strange world, filled with strange people who hurt me. I had just forgotten. I pretended it wasn't there until I was able to forget it entirely. It had been so hard, grabbing hold of my new human reality. I almost went insane. Helen had saved me. Her friendship and sisterhood grounded me and helped me be human.

"You saved my life. You kept that monster Bob away from me and he hurt you." Tears streamed down my face. "You died for me."

She nodded. "You were my baby sister. I loved you and protected you."

"What about Jake? Was he real?"

"Jake is someone I met on the other side. He is a beautiful soul, but I cannot be with him. I thought I could, but I can't. I can't until I am done here."

I shook my head, trying to wrap my mind around all of this.

"What am I?"

"You are one of them. You are one of the old gods. You are the door to the Shadowlands. When the door opens, the darkness will escape. R'yleh will crumble and the gods before time will awaken. You will continue to burn everything in your path until the door opens. You will be wind and fire. You will be water. You are an elemental."

I closed my eyes and imagined fire and when I opened them again my hand was on fire. Helen was right. "He said I was Jane of the Air?" I asked her. "Why am I burning?"

"I think you have many powers. I don't entirely understand, but I think you are a door and you contain much of the power from what is behind the door."

"What? How do I control that?"

Helen shrugged in dismay.

"How do you know all of this? You're a human."

"I see things here on the other side…that is why I came back…to warn you, my dear sister."

I sat down beside Helen. I looked at the tattoos on my arms. They moved and breathed. I reached out and touched Helen. "How do we stop this?" I whispered.

Helen shook her head. "I don't know if we can. I don't think we can stop anything. I just know that you and Edward are important. I know that somehow you two are part of this."

I waited for Helen to say more.

"I know you love Edward, but you have to realize that danger lies ahead. If you go to him, everything will change.

I shook my head. "How can you mean that? I can't leave him."

Helen smiled. "I love you, Jane. I know that I can't stop fate, but you can't blame me for trying. I will see you one day, on the other side."

"Can't you stay?"

"I cannot be in this house. I cannot be here in the way I used to. I am only half here. Cerrus can't know. Don't tell him. I think he is evil. He is worse than the Devil himself…

My eyes filled with tears for my beautiful sister.

"Run away, Jane. Run someplace beautiful and live your life. You don't deserve to hurt anymore. I will see you again one day…"

# CHAPTER 27

*If you gaze long enough into the abyss, the abyss will gaze back at you.*

~ Nietzsche

WHEN I AWOKE, I WENT back to Edward's house and sat by the tree across the street. I watched him through the window. I wanted to cry, but there were no tears for me. I sat until evening came and then I walked home. I tried to eat, but my stomach felt like a rock. There was no room for food, so I showered. In the mirror, I saw horror, not wonders. Helen had called them wonders, but I had trouble believing that the writhing mass of tentacles and mangled flesh, with a thousand eyes and teeth, that was peering out at me from my thigh was anything but a horror. I covered myself in leggings and a giant sweater and wandered around Cerrus's house. I stared in terror at his collection of baby fetuses in formaldehyde. I picked up old fossils he had collected and statues of strange gods that appeared to be from Mesopotamia. He had chipped engravings of Celtic gods that I touched and studied. Cernunnos looked surprisingly like my father. Perhaps my father was Cernunnos.

Finally, I wandered into the library. It was half the size of Thornfield's, but it was set up like a maze. The books that lined the shelves were nothing like Thornfield's books. There were old copies of books on gods and demons. Satanic texts and gnostic gospels, from hundreds of years, ago sat next to scrolls written in Mandarin. One of the books looked like it was bound in flesh. It was a library that was not for a book lover like me. I did not feel happy in there. Finally, I went back to bed.

In the morning, I went back to Edward's house. I spent the week this way. I got less and less sleep. I stopped eating. I wandered between my new home with its cabinet of curiosities and Edward's home, where I sat and stared with longing. A week passed and I still hadn't eaten and sleep had become impossible. I wandered like a ghost.

After my second week there, Cerrus came and sat beside me, outside of Edward's house. We stared up at Edward's windows together. "What are you doing, Jane?" he asked.

"Losing my mind," I answered.

"Come home," he said. "I'll cook you dinner."

I took my father's hand and looked up into his eyes. He was smiling again.

"What is happening to me?" I asked. "I feel like I'm going insane. I feel wrong."

"Come home."

We went back to Cerrus's townhouse and he sat me down in the kitchen and made us dinner. Surprisingly, it was good. There was foie gras on crostini, caviar-filled crepes, and lobster stuffed ravioli in a delicate cream sauce. It was beyond good. It was divine. He even made me dessert. Chocolate mousse so good I closed my eyes and sighed. I ate until I began to feel normal again. After my meal was done, I felt calm for the first time since I had left Huntington. My head cleared and my thoughts came together. I looked down at my hands. Tiny flowers decorated my fingers. Bugs were hiding behind the flowers. They were pretty. I pulled up my sleeve. The monsters were covered in flowers and grass. There was a beauty in it.

"Do you feel better?" Cerrus asked.

I nodded.

"You have to stop this," he said. His perpetual smile faded and his features changed. His eyes turned yellow again. His skin turned dark like wood. Horns grew from his head. I looked down at my skin. We had the same color skin, although mine lacked his texture. "You can't wander around this house and this neighborhood like a ghost."

"I don't want to open the door," I said.

"Why?"

"I don't want to hurt anyone."

"What makes you think it will hurt anyone?" His voice was deeper.

"You are a monster."

"Am I? Maybe *they* are the monsters. Eons ago, before man devoured this world, we ruled. There was no war.

Fathers didn't rape their daughters. We took care of the world. We kept the green spaces and fed the dark oceans. Man imprisoned us. They locked us behind four doors. They are the monsters. I am only a prisoner seeking freedom."

"If I go to him, no one will be hurt?"

Cerrus stood up and kissed my forehead. "You are my most beautiful creation. You were fashioned from love. You could never hurt anyone. There is nothing that is any part of you that could cause any pain to anyone. No one will be hurt."

"Promise?" I wanted to believe Cerrus so badly. I wanted to go to Edward. I felt like I was dying, withering. I felt like I needed Edward. I felt like what I imagined drug addicts felt like when they were going through withdrawal.

"I would never lie to you," Cerrus said.

# CHAPTER 28

*We live on a placid island of
ignorance in the midst of the black
seas of the infinity, and it was not
meant that we should voyage far.*

~ H.P. Lovecraft

THE NEXT MORNING, I WENT back to Edward's
house and sat on the doorstep. I was still afraid to go in. I
waited. I watched the tattoos on my hands and I waited.
Mrs. Fairfax found me.

I was sitting in front of Edward's house, watching it,
and she sat down next to me. "It really is cruel, making an
old lady sit on the ground like this," she said.

"I'm sorry." I blushed. My embarrassing stalking behavior had been noticed.

"What are you doing, Jane?" she asked.

I shrugged. I had no answers that made sense. I just
knew I was tired and worn thin.

"Come inside."

"I can't." My voice was hoarse with emotion.

"You can't just sit on the curb watching us forever," she said. "Edward misses you. Come inside."

I nodded and let Mrs. Fairfax lead me to the only place I knew I shouldn't go. I disregarded Helen's warning and I told myself that my father wouldn't lie. I told myself all of this because I loved Edward too much. Mrs. Fairfax took me inside and brewed me some tea.

"What happened to you?" Mrs. Fairfax asked.

"CPS came for me," I answered. "I am living with an uncle now. He lives a few doors down."

Mrs. Fairfax smiled. She was genuinely happy. "Thank God!" she exclaimed. "You need someone watching out for you. You are too young to be on your own."

I shrugged. I was better off on my own.

"You should go see him," Mrs. Fairfax says. "He wants to see you. He is upstairs. Third bedroom on the right."

As I walked upstairs, I told myself I wouldn't go to him. I told myself that I would just peek in. I would watch him for a minute and I would turn around and leave and never come back. But when I stepped into his room and saw him, I was lost.

Seeing Edward made me draw a deep breath. He had been badly burned and the right side of his face was marred by significant scarring. His eyes were wrapped in bandages and it was clear that he was blind. I felt overwhelmed by guilt. I had done this. I had been the cause of the fire that had burned him. My passion had devoured him. I looked at his burnt and mangled face. It didn't matter. He still left me breathless. It would take more than a few scars to strip

172

him of his beauty. He sat in a chair, in the dark. He didn't seem to be doing anything. He was wearing an old ratty t-shirt and shorts. He had grown a beard. It suited him. I placed my hand on his shoulder.

"Who's there?" he snarled.

"It's me," I answered.

"Jane?" he asked.

"Yes," I whispered.

He stumbled toward me and grabbed me and kissed me with the same force and passion as he always had. He lifted me off my feet and held me. "You came back," he whispered.

"Of course," I answered. "I love you."

"I killed Bertha. I'm burnt beyond recognition. Grandmother died in the fire. Why would you come back?"

I kissed him again. I didn't want to stop. I never wanted to let him go again. My body ached for him. Nothing else mattered. All the madness didn't matter. I had to be with him. "How could I not?" I said. "You are my other half."

With that, he picked me up and carried me to the bed. He stumbled again, but we made it there, despite his bandaged eyes. I took off his shirt and kissed his scarred body and he explored me with his hands. Nothing mattered. Time stood still and I lost my virginity in the dark of Edward's New York townhouse. It hurt. There was blood. It wasn't what I expected nor what I had seen in the movies, but Edward was kind and gentle and told me it would get better with time.

"Can I see your eyes?" I asked when everything was done.

"They are horrible," he said.

"I don't care. Can I see them?"

"Okay. I am supposed to take the bandages off every night and put ointment on them."

I slowly peeled the bandages back and Edward opened his beautiful, blue eyes. I melted like I always had.

He gasped. "I can see!" He grabbed my face and kissed me. "I can see you. Holy shit! I burned my eyes. I am not supposed to see! You are magic, Jane."

He stopped suddenly and looked at me. I was completely naked next to him in the bed. I blushed. I had only been comfortable with my nudity because he was blind. "You are perfect," he said. "You are like a fairy queen."

"Shut up," I said.

"We must look like Beauty and The Beast next to each other," he commented.

"That's what I always thought, except I thought you were Beauty and I was The Beast."

"Everything about you is beautiful, Jane. Everything." He kissed me tenderly and my heart filled with love. Then I saw it. An old key hanging around his neck. "Why are you wearing a key around your neck?"

He looked down and grasped it with one hand. "I found it in a box on your dresser in your room after I returned to Thornfield. I thought you'd forgotten it there after you left." His lips quirked in a bittersweet smile. "I put it on a chain and have been wearing it ever since. I can't explain it, but having it around my neck helped me feel close to you."

I reached out and touched the key. "I've never seen it before…someone else put that key there."

"Maybe Liliana did?" he mused. "Maybe it's meant to open something. A box of letters…I guess we'll never know now since the house is pretty much destroyed."

I sighed. "So many mysteries…I'm tired of mysteries." I stood up and walked toward my clothing, which had been abandoned on the floor.

"Speaking of mysteries," Edward said. "Wow! That is an impressive piece of ink, Jane. I didn't think you were that type of girl, but it only makes you more beautiful."

I panicked and yanked my clothes on in a rush. My shirt went on backward and my pants were inside out. Edward stopped me. "Why are you ashamed?" he asked. "No matter what you wear, no matter what you do, you will always be the most beautiful thing I have ever seen." He took my shirt off and studied me, and I let him. I felt his hands trace the outlines of the tattoo on my back. His fingers caressed my flesh as he examined the massive mangle of monsters and madness that had been etched into my skin.

"This is amazing," he said. "It is so real I can almost see it move."

"I never wanted you to see this."

He wrapped his arms around me. "Why are you ashamed? You should never be ashamed in front of me? When did you get it?"

"I didn't," I began to cry. "I've had it since they found me. It was on my back when I was a little girl. It keeps getting bigger. It's growing. I don't understand what is happening to me. I shouldn't be here. I think I am going crazy. I should go."

I tried to leave but he held me tightly. "I'm not going to let you go ever again," he said in a fierce voice.

I met his blue eyes and they were shining with love. I still had to pinch myself that he loved me.

"You're not crazy. There is nothing about you that is crazy. My entire life had been crazy until the day I met you. That was when everything started making sense."

He leaned down and kissed me with such tenderness I started to cry again. When we pulled away, I gasped. I couldn't believe my eyes. "Edward!" I looked him up and down. "Your scars are gone."

"Shit!" he said as he looked down at his body.

The burns on his face and chest were gone. The scars where Bertha had stabbed him were gone. The cracks on his back were gone. He was perfect.

Without thinking, I grabbed him. I pulled him back to the bed and climbed on top of him. I didn't want to fight it anymore. I was right where I wanted to be. With the only guy I would ever love. I let him study my body as an art student would study a Monet. I let myself stop caring about everything that had been slowly driving me insane. I let myself believe that everything would be all right. I had made love to Edward and nothing had happened. No demons had broken free and burst into our world. It had all been in my head. I made love to him again and the pain was gone. The blood was gone. He felt good. I felt better. I felt complete.

"It is beautiful," he said. "You should never be ashamed of this."

He kissed my back and I closed my eyes. I should leave. I knew that, but I couldn't let go of him. I lay on my stomach and let him kiss my tattoo. I let him touch and explore it as I began to doze off into a blissful sleep.

As I drifted off, I could hear him talking to me. "It is mesmerizing. The monsters are almost beautiful. They seem alive. The door almost seems to be glowing, Jane."

I was almost asleep. I was content. I was trying to ignore him…When it happened there was no pain, at first. There was only shock. A bright light came from my back. I grabbed onto Edward. "What is happening?" I asked. I felt like something was leaking out of my back. I couldn't see what was happening.

"I don't know," Edward said. He had fallen onto the bed beside me and was clutching my hand. His face was painted with terror as he stared at me.

"Help me," I pleaded.

"I don't know how," Edward said in desperation.

From within the doorway on my back, I could feel movement. I could feel something emerging from me. It felt like what I imagined it felt like when a child was born. I wailed in pain. From the corner of my eye, I could see something almost human slither out of my back.

I put my hands over my face. I couldn't watch and, somehow, even glimpsing what was happening made the pain that much more unbearable.

"What the hell?" Edward yelled. He held onto me for grim life. "Jane! I am so sorry! How can I make it stop? I don't know what to do!? Tell me how to help you! Jane!" Edward yelled and I felt him release me. I didn't open my eyes. I curled up in the fetal position and prayed for death. The agony was unbearable and, mercifully, I passed out.

# CHAPTER 29

*To know the truth behind reality
is the greatest burden.*

~ H.P. Lovecraft

I WOKE UP ON WHAT I had to assume was Witching Hill. It looked like the Witching Hill from my dream. I was completely naked and wrapped in Edward's arms. It was daylight and it was unspeakably beautiful. The hill was covered in flowers and butterflies danced from flower to flower. Rabbits sat by my feet and what looked like fairies sat beside the rabbits. I sat up and tried to cover myself, but there was nothing to cover myself with.

Edward awoke with a start. He sat up and grabbed me in a protective gesture. "Where the hell are we?"

"I think we've lost our minds. We are crazy."

"Crazy doesn't feel like this."

I stood up and Edward pulled me back into his arms. "Don't," he said. "Stay here and let me make sure we are alone and safe."

"You aren't alone," a voice said from the shadows.

Cerrus emerged from the darkness like he was made of it. His yellow eyes glowed in daylight. He had horns that looked like antlers he'd had in my dream, and his smile was so bright I could have been blinded by it. He was as much tree as man. His skin was dark and covered with bark. Butterflies surrounded him. He was beautiful. I cowered in Edward's arms.

"Who the fuck are you?" Edward demanded.

"I am Cernunnos. Thank you for opening the door. You have begun to set the old ones free. But there is much work to be done. You have done as you needed to do. Just ask for your reward and it will be given to you."

"What the hell is going on!" Edward bellowed.

"You were born of a curse and Jane was born of magic. Together you have unlocked the power of your destiny. You both have more power than you will ever know, and now I offer you any reward for the part you played in the game."

"What came out of my back?" I asked in desperation.

"My brothers and sisters. Your family. Even now, they are creeping down to the worlds below New York to prepare for what is to come. They are building cities of miracles and beauty. We will show your kind wonders. Your love opened the door. The love of an air spirit and a hollow man, a soulless shadow demon born out of black magic and the daughter of the horned god made love. Despite oceans of suffering between them, in doing so, you gave birth to the three gateways that will set all of the old gods free. The first gateway is Love that defeats all obstacles. The second gateway is Hate that changes a person and corrupts all love. The third gateway is Sorrow, which can lead only to death. You, my darling daughter, were the door. And you, young Edward were the key. The old ones have slept too long. We are restless and hungry." Cernunnos smiled like he was talking about the day he met his wife or the birth of his first child. He sat down in the grass and the fairies climbed onto his shoulders.

"What are the old gods?" Edward asked. He looked so confused.

Cernunnos only smiled. His voice was cold and harsh. "We are the sleeping legion that once ruled this world. We have awoken to retake it. We have many names, but we were here before mankind and we shall be here after mankind. Men will fall to their knees, again, and we shall be the kings of all."

"No," I said.

"It is already done. The first gate is open and the second will open soon. You cannot stop it. Luxovious, Ogmious, and many of the nameless are already free. I am free. It is too late, but you have nothing to fear, gentle daughter. You are a queen here and your hollow prince will be a king. I am here to take care of you. What would you ask as your reward?"

"We want no part of this. Send us home," Edward said.

"As you wish," Cernunnos answered.

Edward and I stood alone in his room, naked and covered in dirt. The tattoo on my back was gone. The door had closed and the key around Edward's neck was gone. Edward had healed. There was no evidence of the terror that had happened to him. For a while, we just stood there, holding each other. We were both shaking and confused.

"Was that real?" he asked.

"Yes," I said. I looked down at my naked body. My tattoos on my arms were gone, too, and my flesh felt foreign. All that remained was the rough outline of a skeletal door on my back. "This is my fault and it is real."

"How can this possibly be your fault?"

"I knew something would happen if I came to you, but I came anyway. I acted like a lovesick fool of a girl."

"I wouldn't have done any different, Jane. I would have set the world on fire to be with you. It felt like there was a rope connecting our hearts and when you left, I started bleeding inside. It felt like I was dying without you. If what that thing said is true, wasn't this inevitable? Aren't you my other half? I am the key, you are the door, and this had to be? It wasn't your fault. You can't blame yourself for what you are."

"Isn't that the excuse of every sicko?"

"This is different and you know it, but it's over now and we can choose what we do from here on out. We can choose to change fate."

We got dressed and sat on the bed. The passion was satiated, but we still clung to each other. "What now?" I asked.

"Now, we have to find the other gateways and make sure they never open," Edward said. "We have to stop this."

"How?" I asked.

Edward shook his head. "I don't know yet, but don't you think that if what that monster said was true, if we were built to be together, we can somehow use the power between us to stop this. If we were the keys to letting the monsters out, can't we be the keys to putting them back?"

I nodded. I looked over at Edward. He was right. I felt different. There was a power between Edward and me. There was a kind of fire between us.

"We just have to find out where to start," Edward said. "We need to know how to use our power and stop this."

I put my head on his shoulder. "I think I know where to start. We have to start in my father's house. We have to find the other doors."

"And we have to find what is nesting beneath the city."

I wasn't afraid anymore. I should have been. I should have been terrified, but it seemed like there was nothing else to fear and, somehow, I knew that the fire between Edward and me was something that even Cerrus, the horned god, would fear.

*To be continued...*

# ABOUT JESSICA PENOT

I'm a therapist and a mom. I live in Huntsville, Alabama with my kids, husband, dogs, cats, and other strange creatures. When I'm not writing, I'm probably exploring a haunted house somewhere with my husband and kids, or sharing pictures on Instagram of some cool, scary thing I just bought.

I hope you're enjoying my YA/NA paranormal series called the Tattooed Girl Series inspired by Charlotte Brontë's beloved classic novel, *Jane Eyre*.

The Tattooed Girl Series includes the following books:

*Jane of Air (Book 1)*
*Jane of Fire (Book 2)*
*Jane of Water (Book 3)*
*Jane of Earth (Book 4)*
*Jane of Darkness (Book 5)*
*Jane of Light (Book 6)*

Sign up for my newsletter: Scary Girl News, and follow me on BookBub and Amazon to find out about my new releases and recommendations of books that I love. You can also find out more about me and my books and my spooky blog about real-life hauntings on my website: jessicapenot.com.